Deadman's Pocket

Shirley Manis

Text copyright © 2021 by Shirley Manis

Cover and book design by Daniel Saenz

All right reserved. This print book, or parts thereof, may not be reproduced in any form, by any means, electronic or mechanical, or by any information storage and retrieval system without written permission from the author.

The scanning, uploading and distribution of this book via the Internet or via any other means without permission of the author is illegal and punishable by law.

Please purchase only authorized editions, and do not participate in or encourage piracy of copyrighted materials. Your support of the author's rights is appreciated.

All rights reserved.

ISBN: ISBN 978-0-9839286-3-8
10 9 8 7 6 5 4 3

Other Books by Shirley Manis

Ador the Giant

In a Scoop of Dirt: How Digging a Pond Changed North America's Prehistory

Contents

1	The Unforgettable Day	1
2	What is RBC?	8
3	From Baseball to Trouble	16
4	A Big Dilemma	24
5	Dad's Orders	28
6	A New Dilemma	32
7	Orchestra Rehearsal	36
8	Two Big Dilemmas	42
9	The Comic Book	46
10	Perfect Plan Revealed	53
11	Spying	59
12	The Phone Call	66
13	How to Choose	70
14	Who is the Leader?	77
15	Chimpanzees	81
16	Ropes and Somersaults	86
17	The Rotting Log	91
18	Did I Kill Again?	97
19	Breaking the Rules	99

20 Out of the Blue	105
21 Brothers	111
22 4th of July	116
Epilogue	124
Elliot: In His Own Words	125
Jace: In His Own Words	130

Acknowledgments

Every author owes thanks to those who helped create a book. Much appreciation goes to Martha Bratton for her skillful editing; a special thank you to Evan Griffith, my teen manuscript reviewer, for his advice and feedback; and thanks to Susan Forrest and Dorothy Wise, both of my writing group. Many thanks go to Daniel Saenz, a creative designer, for launching my books into cyberspace.

1
The Unforgettable Day

"Look out below!" Billy Martin sailed off the rock ledge, knees to chest, and disappeared.

I leaned forward and my stomach flipped. The drop to the swimming hole was like falling from a freeway overpass.

Kah-thunk! Billy landed dead center, a perfect cannonball. Within seconds, his head bobbed up through the foamy surface near Skip, my best friend.

I had a bird's-eye view. The once majestic oak lay toppled and rotting above the deep water of the swimming hole. Along the banks, bushes fought for sunlight and space to grow between the jagged rocks and boulders. It was a perfect playground.

"What are you waiting for, Elliot?" Billy gave a stiff-wristed wave. "If I can, anybody can!" He was the smallest among us, with the biggest smile. He was right. I could do this.

I curled my toes over the sharp rock edge. Suddenly, I didn't feel so brave. I swallowed hard. I was supposed to be home practicing my violin solo for the 4th of July concert, but I had to jump off the ledge today. It had been a sixth grade tradition as far back as anyone in Taftsville, Vermont, could remember. If I wanted to hang out with all the other older boys, I couldn't chicken out.

"Come on," urged Capster, the all-star athlete. "Hold your nose like I do sometimes, and jump!"

"Now or never, Ell," Skip urged, as if he could read my thoughts.

I inched further out. Then bushes rustled behind me. I turned, teetering off balance. My older brother Jace charged out, lunged and gave me a brutal two-handed shove. I tumbled downward. My chest smacked the water, hard. I snarfed up gallons of water. When my ears cleared I heard the whoops of my friends. I'd landed a perfect belly flop.

Billy swam over. "You did it!"

"Yeah, and freakin' graceful, too!" Jace taunted from above, standing with his buddy Duke. "You'll have to teach me how to do that, Squeaky."

I hated that nickname. Hearing it made my face feel hotter than the July heat. Jace always took swipes at me. "I'll get you for that," I hollered, even though I didn't exactly know how.

"Oo-oo, I'm r-r-really scared," Jace laughed. He and Duke jumped off the ledge. Their double cannonballs sent so much water flying I couldn't see a thing.

Billy wiped his eyes. "Hey guys, call it before you jump."

"I'll remember that," Duke said as he dunked him.

Billy popped up, sputtering.

I splashed the bully. "Bug off."

Duke curled his lip and spat a stream of water at me.

"You guys ready for some real action?" Jace shouted. "Let's go run the log." He rolled over and dug quick backstrokes, signaling a race. His foamy trail led to the rotting oak that straddled the swimming hole.

Duke, Capster and Skip disappeared in a flume of white splashes. Billy and I hung back. Jumping off the ledge was bad enough, but that deeper, dark water under the log was another story.

Jace climbed the tangled roots – King of the Hill again – and pointed at Billy and me. "Hey, you two are really slow."

Duke stood next to Jace after he'd elbowed past Skip and Capster, who were cranking arm circles to get us to hurry.

"Ignore my brother, Billy. He can't make us go if we don't want to."

Billy kept treading water, but I could see his brain gears turning.

"Screw it," Billy said. "I'm gonna try." He paddled off, breathing and blowing.

I swam after him.

When Billy and I reached the log's root ladder, I gave him a butt boost. I clambered up, hoping not to get splinters in my hands from the bug-infested wood. I stood with Billy.

Jace ran his fingers over his slicked-down hair. "Here's the deal. Run as fast as you can out to that branch stub then jump off in a crazy pose before you hit the water. Watch me!"

Jace flew across the log, leaped high, stretched out his legs and touched his toes, hitting the water in a sitting V-position. Duke dashed to the stub, somersaulted forward at an angle, landing upside down in a tight ball, making a huge spray of water. Capster soared in a spastic swan dive. He didn't even hold his nose! Skip's fancy footwork ended when he slipped off halfway out. He landed backward on top of Jace, Duke and Capster. A water fight broke out.

Who could top them? A pale Billy swayed and said, "Maybe I don't want to do this after all."

Jace appeared behind me for another run. "Move it! We don't have all day!"

I turned and stabbed my index finger into Jace's shoulder. "Back off!" He brushed my hand away as if I was an annoying bug. Then he shoved me back for the second time that day. So, I coiled and swung my fist. A surprised look crossed his face. He ducked and dove sideways into the water fight still raging below. Coming around, I barreled full-speed into Billy. I was unable to keep my balance.

Billy lurched forward, wobbling wildly. He stuck his thumbs in his armpits, flapped his elbows like a bird, and staggered along the wet log trying to get his balance.

The water war halted when everyone noticed Billy. "Go Billy!"

"Sorry!" I called after him. "I didn't mean to...."

Billy flashed me a cockeyed grin and opened his mouth to say something. Instead, he tripped and fell face first against the branch stub.

Smack!

He lay spread-eagled over the log, unmoving. Everything went silent. Even the birds stopped chirping.

Somebody called, "Billy?"

His arm jerked. One leg slowly slid off the log, followed by the other. His body dangled by his head for a moment, as if the tree didn't want to let go, then Billy plopped into the water.

"Guys! Guys, do something!" I screamed and went further out onto the log. The mossy wood was as slippery as snot on a stick, but I managed to remain upright. I pointed at the bubbles. "Hey, he went down there!"

A few inches from my toes was the stub, covered with blood. Billy's red blood.

Jace and Duke swam as fast as they could and dove under where Billy had disappeared. They surfaced, gasping for air, but no Billy. They dove again. Seconds later, the three bobbed up. Jace and Duke struggled to keep Billy's flopping head above water. I backtracked on the log and climbed down the roots. Capster and Skip swam toward shore. They dragged the blue-faced kid onto the pebbly shore and laid him on his back.

Billy's left eyeball had been drilled into his head. Blood oozed from his eye socket, trickling into his ears and onto the ground.

"Billy? Billy?" Skip shook him a couple of times.

He'd wake up in a second. He had to.

"Somebody do CPR!" Capster cried out.

"I'll call 9-1-1," Duke yelled, fumbling for his cell in the clothes he left in the bushes.

Everyone started yelling at once. We scurried around like football players without a strategy. Jace knelt down and put his ear against Billy's motionless chest. My brother's lips quivered. Then Jace crumpled in shock, staring into space.

"I can't believe this happened," Capster hollered. "It was just a stupid game." He swiped at his tears. "Nobody was supposed to get hurt."

Skip marched around in circles, saying, "Oh, God! Oh, God!" Then he dropped on all fours and puked.

Shirley Manis

Still dazed, Jace reached for his beach towel and covered Billy's face. Duke joined him. I rocked back and forth. What had I done?

2
What is RBC?

I watched the video clip I saved on my cell of Billy over and over. The paper said it was an accident, but I knew differently. It still didn't seem real. I just wanted Jace to shut up so Billy could make a good jump. If I hadn't lost my temper and swung at Jace, Billy would be alive.

I didn't go to Billy's funeral. Instead, I laid on my bed and stared at the ceiling. Just before Mom, Dad and Jace left, Jace tossed me a box of tissues, and said, "Staying home won't bring him back." I knew that.

For two weeks after the funeral, I didn't leave the house and practiced my violin solo furiously to block out that day. But I couldn't stop thinking about Billy. How he'd raced around the baseball diamond and whistled from across the playground. How he made those quirky stiff-wristed waves. How he yelled, "Look out below!" before someone sailed off the rock ledge. Day and night my brain replayed Billy's last run on the rotting oak.

Later while I was practicing, Dad's voice boomed from downstairs, "Skip just rode up on his bike. Come down."

"I'm busy!" I shouted.

Mom appeared in my doorway. "Put your violin away. You need to get out and be with your friends. Enough sulking."

I dragged myself downstairs with Mom close behind.

Skip drummed a rhythm impatiently on the door. *Bum bum-pa dum-dum...bum bum.*

"Go ahead, let him in," urged Mom, turning toward the kitchen. "I'll get some sodas."

I cracked open the door.

Skip pushed it wide and shoved his sunglasses up onto his head. "Where've you been hiding?"

I shrugged, leading the way into the kitchen.

Mom set two sweaty soda cans on the table.

"Thanks, Mrs. Wermann," Skip popped his tab, chugged, then let out a belch.

"Ugh, gross." I rolled my eyes.

"Oops, sorry." Skip took another swig, but swallowed the next burp. "I heard Capster called a baseball game today. He said we're playing in Billy's honor. Seems the right thing to do after the accident."

Accident nothing. Skip had been in the water war and hadn't seen me barrel into Billy, forcing his final run. I took a slow sip and mumbled, "Don't feel like it."

"The fresh air will do you good," said Mom. "You've done enough practicing for one day."

I shot her a pleading look.

"Yeah, Ell." Skip jumped up and lifted the cookie jar lid, which was empty. "Got any other snacks, Mrs. Wermann?"

Skip always poked around our kitchen searching for food. Mom often asked me if his parents ever fed him. She gave me *the look*. I knew it was time to go.

"Okay...I'll get my mitt and meet you out front," I said half-heartedly.

Skip waved at Mom and pulled his sunglasses down onto his nose. "Thanks for the soda, Mrs. Wermann."

We took off. Skip led the way. We passed through the stone pillars at the entrance into Jasper Lawton Ipes Park, named for the first Taftsville mayor. Pedaling past swings, sandboxes and teeter-totters, we reached the baseball diamond. The blinding white baselines had just been chalked and the outfield lawn freshly mowed.

"Over here! Look at this!" Capster waved his New York Yankees ball cap like a lunatic fan. He stood with Reggie, the school brainiac, at the backstop.

We leaned our bikes against a tree and ran up to the hand-printed sign hanging on the fence.

> RBC
>
> IF YOU GOT ANY GUTS
>
> COME TO THE SWIMMING HOLE
>
> NEXT SAT. - ONE O'CLOCK SHARP
>
> ABSOLOOTLY NO GIRLS ALLOWED

We all stared at it. I recognized that lousy spelling.

It took a second for Reggie to ask the question aloud. "What's RBC?" He cleaned his glasses with a corner of his T-shirt. "Whatever it is, I'm not permitted to play at the swimming hole any longer due to, you know…."

"Me, neither." Capster put on his cap. "My parents will lock me up if I get caught there."

Skip sunk his fist in his pocket, pulled out some bubble gum, unwrapped it and popped it in his mouth. "Same for me."

I wasn't supposed to go there either, and no one had to ban me. I didn't want to go.

"What a bunch of losers!" That grating voice behind us belonged to Jace.

"Do you know what RBC is?" asked Capster, turning his ball cap backwards, putting himself into concentration mode. That's how he got his cool nickname.

Jace nodded.

"Well?" asked Capster, stabbing Skip's pink bubble. "Spill."

"It stands for River Boys Club." Jace swaggered around us. "Saturday after next, we'll sneak down to Deadman's Pocket—,"

Skip sucked in his deflated bubble. "Deadman's Pocket?"

Jace leaned into him until they were nose to nose. "The swimming hole, stupid! I named it Deadman's Pocket—for Billy."

"You think Billy'd like that?" asked Skip between slobbery chomps.

Jace stared him down.

Skip backed up. "Great name."

"Billy loved that place," said Jace, "and would've wanted us to keep playing there."

Where did Jace get off preaching about what Billy wanted? He'd barely ever said two words to the kid, except for his mean teasing.

"Only the toughest will be allowed to join," said Jace. "Those who don't pass the contests will be losers."

"Except no one's allowed to use the swimming—uh, er, Deadman's Pocket anymore," said Reggie.

"Says who?" Jace stood taller.

Reggie's eyes widened.

I wasn't surprised. Jace didn't care about rules, anyone's rules, except his.

Jace turned to me. "Hey Squeaky, don't think just because we're related, you're getting a free pass."

Who cared? No way I'd go back to that swimming hole for RBC or anything else. I wish he'd stop calling me Squeaky. I've learned to play the violin and my beginner squeaky days are over.

"Hey, did you see it? They put up a fence blocking the path we used to the rock ledge," said Capster, bringing his cap brim around forward. "Won't the park caretaker, Mr. Pazaropoulos, call the cops if we jumped over it?"

I couldn't believe Capster was actually considering this.

Jace folded his arms across his chest. "Piece of cake. When Mr. P zooms around on that noisy lawn mower every Saturday he'll be far from that fence. He's half deaf anyway."

Capster nodded like he'd thought of that himself.

"Come on, Squeaky. Dare ya to go back to the scene," taunted my brother with a sneer.

I clenched my fists, held my breath, then exhaled the words, "I can't."

"You mean you won't."

I was close enough to spit in his eye, but my mouth was too dry. "No, I can't. I have orchestra rehearsals on Saturdays."

Jace danced around and clucked like a chicken. "Lame reason, Squeaky. Tryouts take real talent."

What did Jace know about talent? Jace couldn't even keep the beat with a tambourine. "You know I have a solo."

Jace hooked his thumbs in his jeans and looked my friends up and down. "What about you guys? The rock ledge, my surprise event, and...the log. RBC will be crazy fun!"

Fun? Not for me. Maybe Jace was right. Maybe I was a chicken. But even if I wanted to try out for RBC, I couldn't.

"So, who's coming?"

No one answered.

"You girls need skirts!" Jace ripped the sign from the fence, spun around and sprinted off the field.

Reggie broke the silence. "Those contests sound rather challenging."

"Brutal is more like it," said Capster, warming up with a few jumping jacks. "I wonder what his surprise event is going to be?"

"Guess we'll know in a couple of weeks," said Skip. Then he looked at me. "I mean, if anyone goes."

An awkward silence hung in the air. Were all my friends going to go and risk getting caught? If they made it and became River Boys and I didn't, I'd be a loser like Jace said.

"Let's play ball for Billy!" said Capster, sounding overly cheerful.

Playing baseball in Billy's honor was all I could do for him now. If only I'd nailed that punch at Jace on the log, Billy would be here. But I missed.

3
From Baseball to Trouble

"Yo, buddy," yelled Capster, pointing at me. "You're up. I'll pitch."

Skip played all the bases. Reggie sprinted to the outfield. But it wasn't the same without Billy. He was our ace catcher.

My turn didn't take long. One, two, three, out. After me, Skip slugged a line drive. Even Reggie got a base hit. Why couldn't I hit the stupid thing? I was lucky they let me play at all. Then Capster walked over, handed me the ball and told me to pitch. Guess he thought I'd drop the ball if he tossed it to me.

Capster waited at home plate, rocking from one foot to the other like any good New York Yankee. "Make it a good one!"

I concentrated, aimed, then threw. I pitched a wild one, but Capster swung and smacked it hard. The ball sailed across the sun toward Reggie.

"Run! Run!" a screaming voice boomed from the metal bleachers.

I spun around. It was Marcy Bettencourt, the only neighborhood girl who could pitch, catch and hit a home run. She played violin, too, though not as well as me.

"Need a pitcher?" bellowed Marcy, punching the pocket of her mitt, shooting me an *I-saw-that-lousy-pitch look.*

"Get lost, Missy Redhead!" yelled Capster. "Boys only."

"Yeah!" shouted Skip.

"You know I can pitch better than Elliot," argued Marcy.

"Beat it!" Capster swatted a buzzing fly. "It's my turn to pitch."

"We abide by strictest of rules," said Reggie.

"Rules for idiots." Marcy climbed off the bleachers. "As long as I can hit and pitch, who cares?"

Skip shot me a look that said *get rid of her.*

I had to think fast. "Sorry Marcy, we're finished," I slapped the dust off my cargo shorts. "The sun's way too hot."

She stamped her feet. "So, why are you all still standing there? Come on. I oiled my mitt, I'm ready and you need another player."

I kicked at the dirt with my sneakers, searching for something else to say to make her leave.

"Afraid I might show you up, Elliot?" taunted Marcy.

We all knew she could beat me at baseball any day of the week. Since she wasn't leaving, we ignored her.

"Next batter!" Skip pointed at me.

I stood at home plate, gripping the bat with white knuckles.

"Hey batter-batter, hey batter-batter-batter," chanted Marcy, messing with my head.

Capster pitched the first ball. I swung and missed.

"Strike one!" called Marcy.

"Never mind her," shouted Skip. "Concentrate!"

Another slow pitch and I misjudged that one, too. On my last swing, I popped a high-flying foul ball. It sailed back over my head.

Marcy reached up and caught it smack in the middle of her glove. "Strike three. You're out!" She whirled around, tossed the mitt and the ball into her handlebar basket then sped off. Her bike tires spit dust and gravel. "See ya at rehearsal, Champ!"

"Hey, that's my ball," shouted Capster but she was long gone.

* * *

Back home, I hung my bike on overhead hooks in the garage. Dad insisted on keeping things organized. I unlaced my dusty sneakers and left them at the door. Then I slipped in my stocking feet as I rounded the corner into the utility room.

"Moron," said Jace, leaning against the washing machine and taking off his T-shirt.

"Shut up." I tossed my sweaty socks at the laundry basket...and missed. I never threw anything while he watched, but I really thought I'd nailed it.

Jace rolled his eyes.

"Double shut up." I stepped up to wash my face and pits at the sink. Snatching a folded towel from the clean pile, I caught a whiff of Jace. "Ugh! Where've you been?"

"What's it to you?" He turned his back on me.

I spied a wet leaf in his greasy hair. His soggy jeans smelled like stale river water. "Ah-ha! Down at the swimming hole with Duke?"

"Yeah, so? What of it?"

Duke was a magnet for trouble, especially when he hung around with Jace. One night last month, I saw Jace climb out of his bedroom window. The two jerks toilet-papered Principal West's front yard maple tree, then set fire to the leftover rolls in the street. They sprayed "prinsipole sux" in white paint on his black curbside mailbox. The newspaper reported the incident the next day, saying Taftsville's fire truck and two cop cars had roared up to the curb, lights flashing, only to find a tiny pile of smoldering ashes and the wet graffiti. Jace should count himself lucky I never told. I didn't need any more of his wrath. Mom would just tell him to wait until Dad got home. Then Dad would ground him, either making him clean the toilets or be on kitchen patrol. Mom always welcomed the extra help.

"What's that RBC surprise you mentioned?" Not that I cared. I just wanted to leak the news to Skip.

My brother shoved past me. "What's it to you, Squeaky? You're too chicken for the tryouts."

"I'm not a chicken." My voice cracked.

Jace laughed. "Stick to your violin."

I closed my fist and swung just as Mom walked in. Jace dodged. My white knuckles slammed into her flowered wallpaper.

"How awful!" Mom rushed over and took my hand, inspecting both sides. "You mustn't injure those fingers."

I yanked it away and cradled my throbbing fist.

Jace mimicked Mom's voice. "Mustn't hurt yourself."

"Stop it, Jason!" Mom ordered. She paused to look him over. "Where did you get so wet?"

I was about to open my mouth, but Jace's pursed lips made me think twice.

Mom poured detergent into the washer and walked off toward the kitchen, calling over her shoulder. "Jason, toss in your filthy clothes and start the machine."

"Yeah, okay, okay." Jace stripped and jammed his jeans into the washer. He jiggled the knobs that often got stuck until the wash cycle kicked on, then dropped the lid with a bang. As he passed by, he drilled an elbow into my chest and whispered, "You're pathetic and you know it."

But I'd guessed right about the swimming hole. So much for Jace's secret.

"A-hole!" I yelled.

"That's enough!" Mom's voice echoed from the kitchen. "I won't have that language in this house!"

"Jace started it." I argued. "He always does! If Dad was here, he'd...."

"Fix the damn washer knobs?" Jace hollered back.

"Jason Wermann," said Mom in a threatening tone.

We both fell silent. Calling us by our full names meant we were one word away from punishment. Jace tromped upstairs. I plopped down at the kitchen table with a big sigh and cleared my throat a few times.

"Sore throat?" asked Mom, peeling potatoes at the sink.

"No."

"How was your game today?"

"Fine." I cleared my throat again.

"So what's the problem?" asked Mom.

"Jace went down to the river today."

Mom dropped the potato peeler and turned around. "How do you know?"

"Mom, he stunk—big time."

"He should start using deodorant," said Mom.

"No, I mean he reeked like river water."

"Now that you mention it...."

The phone rang. She dried her hands while I grabbed an ice cube for my sore fist. She listened a while. I heard her tell Dad that Jace had gone to the swimming hole today. She hung up the phone. "Jason!"

I chuckled to myself. Couldn't wait to see him get into trouble.

"Jason!" called Mom again.

"Wha-a-at?" Jace finally answered from the top of the stairs. "I was in the shower."

"Get down here right now!"

He showed up, wet hair dripping blotches on his black T-shirt.

"What were you doing down at the river?" asked Mom.

"Who said I was there?"

"Doesn't matter who. Were you?" Mom's eyebrows knitted tighter as she waited. He sneered at me.

"Answer me!" She rested a fist on one hip.

"Uh –,"

"Your father and I told you to stay away from that dangerous place. Why did you go there?" Pretending he didn't hear the question, Jace eyed a bag of chips on the counter. He rammed a fistful into his mouth as he opened the fridge, grabbed the milk and guzzled straight from the jug.

Mom snatched it away. "We share this milk, young man!" The veins in her neck bulged like blue earthworms. "Let's have it, Jason, the truth!"

I sat quietly, itching for the punishment he deserved.

"Okay, yeah. I was."

She only paused long enough to suck in her breath and yell, "You've really stepped over the line this time. Your father will deal with you when he gets home! Go to your room!"

Jace glowered at me.

I smiled sweetly. Gotcha!

4
A Big Dilemma

Mom clanged her pots and pans in the kitchen louder than usual as she made dinner. Hip-hop music blared from my brother's room. I crawled into my bedroom closet to escape the ruckus and fingered my solo on an imaginary violin.

Once again, Jace was in the hot seat. Thanks to me. How would Dad punish Jace this time? I couldn't wait.

Whenever Dad got mad, he turned into a drill sergeant. Mom said he was so strict because of his years in the military. So what would Jace get— a year at a juvenile delinquent camp? Fat chance. He was Dad's favorite, maybe because his room looked like a soldier's quarters. Dad could bounce a quarter off Jace's bed, and that made him happy. My room looked like the aftermath of a tornado.

Dad and Jace often played football and baseball together, but never with me, probably because I couldn't catch anything. Today I confirmed I couldn't even toss a pair of sweaty socks into the laundry basket. So what? I couldn't risk hurting my hands. But I couldn't understand how Jace could be Dad's favorite when my brother was always getting into deep trouble. And, I hadn't ratted on Jace yet for smoking under the Ipes Park bleachers with Duke.

Mom understood me the most. She was first chair in an orchestra when she was my age, so she knew the effort I put into it.

I heard Skip's ringtone above the racket. I found my cell and answered. He lived next door, but he still liked to call.

"Want to ride bikes?" asked Skip.

"Naw. It's almost time to eat."

"What's your Mom fixin'?"

I started to answer, but caught myself. Definitely not a good night for Skip to invite himself to dinner. "Liver and onions!" I blurted out as the yummy smell of chicken stir-fry drifted into my room.

"I'll pass," said Skip, pretending to gag. "Have you thought any more about Jace's club?"

"No."

"It would be so cool since you've already jumped off the rock ledge. One scary part over."

"Yeah, but I don't want to go back there."

"Why not?" Skip was silent for a moment then said, "What happened to Billy wasn't your fault, you know. Anyone could have slipped off the log. I've done it myself."

He hadn't seen me crash into Billy, which forced him to move before he was ready. Then a

Deadman's Pocket

flash of Billy's mutilated face appeared before my eyes. "I can't. I just can't."

"Well, I'm going."

"Fine." That came out meaner than I wanted.

"Oh, come on!" said Skip. "You're not the only one who misses Billy. We all do, and we all need to go back to face our bad memories of that place. It's the only way. Like getting back up on your bike after a fall. We'll go together, you and me, okay?"

My face got hot. "Even if I wanted to, I can't," I said. "My orchestra rehearsal."

"So, be a no-show."

It was tempting. But I had a solo. If I missed the final rehearsal, Miss O'Looney would kick me out of the concert altogether. And, this one was extra special – the 4th of July dedication for the new gazebo at Jasper Lawton Ipes Park. Then again, if I did go to the RBC tryouts, Jace might quit calling me a loser or the dozen other names he and Duke used.

I opened and closed my mouth—twice—before I whispered. "I'll think about it."

"Great!"

"But I'd need to find a way to get out of rehearsal." I said.

"How about this? I'll pretend to be your mother and call Miss O' and tell her you're sick. Then you'll have an *excused* absence."

"Who'd be dumb enough to believe you're my mom? Give me time to figure something out." I rocked back on my heels. To change the subject, I said, "Hey, did I tell you Jace was down at the river today with Duke? When I got home from our game he was soaked in river water. Then he ticked me off, so I nailed him good."

"How?" asked Skip.

"I told my Mom where he'd been."

"You ratted him out to your mother?" Skip slapped his forehead loud enough for me to hear over the phone. "What planet are you on?"

"He deserved it."

"Maybe so, but Jace will get back at you for that," warned Skip. "What did your Mom do?"

"Nothing," I said. "She said Dad would deal with Jace when he gets home from work."

"Uh-oh, now my mom is calling me. Gotta go." Skip hung up.

I mulled things over. What if I actually did go with Skip for RBC? I could lose my solo and fail at the tryouts? Then I'd be a double loser. My stomach churned. Suddenly, I lost my appetite, even for stir-fry.

5
Dad's Orders

"Elliot! Jason!" called Mom. "Dinner's ready!"

I walked into the kitchen. Jace pushed past me and pinched my back—a nail digging, twisting kind of pinch.

"Jerk!" I squirmed and flailed an elbow at him.

"Cool it, boys," said Dad with pursed lips.

I slipped into my chair, watching Jace's every move. No one spoke while Mom ladled stir-fry over a mountain of rice with a triple portion for Dad. When she finally sat down, Jace leaned forward, his chin a couple inches from his plate, and shoveled. I fidgeted with my food, waiting to see what Dad would do. I glanced across the table and caught one of Jace's famous stares. If he had lasers for eyes, I'd have a hole drilled through my forehead.

As Dad ate, his cheek muscles flexed. He cleaned off his plate and drained his water glass, then broke the silence. "Jason." His tone meant sparks were about to fly. "You are forbidden to go to the swimming hole, correct?"

"Yes, Sir," said Jace, squirming, and not looking up.

"Stay away from there."

That was it? Stay away? Where was his extraordinary punishment?

"Why me?" whined Jace. "I've played there a lot and nothing has ever happened."

Dad wadded up his napkin and threw it on his empty plate. "Doesn't matter. Now something has happened. That place is still off limits. That's an order."

"I'm fourteen," argued Jace, turning red-faced. "I don't see anything wrong with hanging out there. Quit treating me like a baby."

Dad stood up and thumped Jace's arm. With a seriously deep voice, he said, "Then stop acting like one."

I took a bite of food to hide my smile. Jace rubbed his arm muscle.

"Kenneth, please." Mom reached for Jace, but he moved out of her reach. She never liked it when Dad raised a hand toward us. "Jason, we just want you to be safe. Accidents won't happen if kids don't go there."

Dad turned and pointed his index finger straight at me. "And don't you get any bright ideas about going there, either. Are we clear on this?"

I nodded furiously.

Dad sat down, leaned back and folded his arms across his chest. He looked like a combat-ready Marine, fit and trim, biceps bulging under his khaki green T-shirt. "Soon, it won't matter.

My buddy Nick got the contract to chop up that nuisance log."

"What?" I gawked at Dad. As he turned toward me I morphed my face into a smile. "A-1 idea, Sir."

"Thank goodness," said Mom, lifting her eyes toward heaven as she took the dirty plates to the sink. "When?"

"Next Wednesday," said Dad, pushing back his chair. That meant it was okay to leave the table, so I stood, too. "Once that old rotten oak dries out it will make good firewood."

Jace mumbled, "Blah, blah, whatever."

Uh-oh. Jace didn't know when to quit.

Dad narrowed his eyes. "Head to your bunk, cadet."

Jace scraped his chair back and stomped upstairs like he was wearing lead boots.

Dad shouted, "You're grounded for a week!"

Jace slammed his bedroom door.

"Make it two weeks, so you can learn to show some respect," called Dad.

I went to my room and stretched out on my bed. If I hadn't pointed out the evidence, Mom wouldn't have caught Jace. Score one for me. But I never expected the log to get hacked up. Between that and Dad banning us from the swimming hole, Jace would have to call off the RBC tryouts.

No more mumbo jumbo about facing ghosts of Billy. Now I could go to my rehearsal and not miss a thing. Cool.

6
A New Dilemma

Since I was early for my mid-week rehearsal at the school cafeteria, I detoured through Ipes Park. Something hanging on the baseball diamond backstop caught my eye. I skidded to a stop, set down my violin case and leaned my bike against the tree. There hung a wrinkled, yet familiar, sign. This time, it read:

> RBC
>
> IF YOU GOT ANY GUTS
>
> COME TO ~~THE SWIMMING HOLE~~
>
> DEADMAN'S POCKET
>
> ~~NEXT~~ SAT. - ONE O'CLOCK SHARP
>
> ABSOLOOTLY NO GIRLS ALLOWED

Was Jace crazy? He was going through with RBC and had moved up the tryouts by a week! But he'd been grounded. How did he expect to duck out on Dad? And how did his sign get here? I bet Duke posted it. I heard some yelling and whooping. Skip, Capster, and Reggie zoomed up behind me.

"Ell, you okay?" asked Skip.

I stood straighter. "Yeah, why?"

"You look rather distressed at the moment," said Reggie.

"Gee, thanks." I grumbled.

Capster pointed at the sign. "Why'd Jace change to this Saturday?"

I shrugged. "Simple. My dad's buddy got hired to chain saw the oak next week on Wednesday. This is the only Saturday before the oak becomes history."

"Obliterating the hazard," said Reggie, pushing up his glasses with his index finger. "One way to save lives."

I wiped my forehead. "I'd better go to rehearsal on Saturday anyway."

"Wait a minute, dude," said Skip, smelling of bubblegum. "Yesterday you promised to go with me."

"No, I didn't. I said I'd think about it."

"Come on, you have to." Skip rubbed his palms together. "This is our chance. Don't you see? Jace knows it, too. If we return there before the log is gone, we'll conquer Deadman's Pocket. It'll be awesome, you'll see."

I stared at Skip without speaking. The pause was so long that someone could've run the whole diamond before anyone spoke.

"I agree," said Capster. "The thought of going back gives me the creeps, but Skip's got a point. If we don't go, we'll be losers and never know how brave we could be. Get it?"

Reggie sighed, wringing his hands. "Since you presented it like that, I suppose we all should venture forth."

Their reasons did make some sense. Even though I didn't want to go, I knew Skip was right. I had to go. Otherwise Billy's face would haunt me forever.

"So are we united?" asked Skip. "One for all and all for one?" He stretched out his hand, palm down.

Capster flipped his Yankee ball cap around and slapped his hand on top of Skip's, followed by Reggie. They stared at me, waiting.

"You with us?" asked Skip.

I exchanged glances with them. "It's got to be our secret, though. No one can breathe a word, or my Dad will—"

"Okay, done," said Skip, pulling an imaginary zipper across his mouth.

Suddenly, my phone alarm buzzed. I pulled it out of my pocket. "Geez, I've got rehearsal in ten minutes." I raced toward my bike and violin.

"Hey, hand or no hand on the pile, you're in," shouted Capster.

Skip followed me. "I'll ride with you."

We pedaled quickly. On the way, Skip repeated how happy he was that I decided to tryout with him.

I parked my bike outside the cafeteria, and groaned. "I'd rather eat a frog than ask Miss O' to let me out of rehearsal."

Skip scratched his head. "Who knows, she might surprise you and say okay."

That was a possibility. After tryouts there was still one final rehearsal before the 4th of July concert. On the other hand, she might completely flip out. My sweaty fingers felt glued to my violin case. She was already a nervous wreck and getting loopier at every practice. "Okay, I'll ask her today."

"You won't know till you ask. Go for it!"

Skip's big grin gave me courage. I locked my bike, praying Miss O' would be in a good mood.

As I opened the cafeteria door, she was screaming at the top of her lungs.

7
Orchestra Rehearsal

"People, people!" shouted Miss O'Looney, tapping her baton on her music stand. "Attention, please!"

I scrambled to get ready. A jumble of instrument cases lined the walls. Miss O' had invited her students from two other middle schools to practice with us. The cafeteria was extra crowded and hotter than an oven.

Miss O' had made me concertmaster last year after Teddy Robinson's family moved away. She assigned Marcy Bettencourt second chair, right next to me. Marcy thought she was the best violinist in all of Vermont's student orchestras. I searched the room. Where was she, anyway?

"People!" The teacher pulled out a handkerchief from her pocket, snapped it open and dabbed her forehead dry. She tapped her toe, waiting for silence. "Let's tune our instruments."

I held my violin at attention. The room grew quiet.

"Finally. Thank you," Miss O' said. "Now, here's the your note." She pointed to me and winked. I drew the bow across my violin. She had told me that my perfect pitch was a gift.

After everyone finished tuning, she said, "Our first piece will be *Stars and Stripes Forever*. Remember the key of E flat has three flats: E, A and B." Papers rustled. Miss O' raised her arms like an eagle about to take flight.

Marcy slipped into the chair beside me, jostling our music stand. She smiled a witch-like grin.

I hissed out of the corner of my mouth. "Where'd you park your broom?"

"Nice of you to show up, Miss Bettencourt."

Marcy lowered her head and sprouted a half-grin.

Again, the teacher raised her baton and gave the upbeat. We didn't start together, but we barreled onward.

"No, no!" she shrieked, trying to stop her runaway musicians. "I'm not waving my baton to kill flies. Watch me!" She snatched her handkerchief and patted her glistening forehead again. "Take it from the top. And Emily, you missed the E flat."

I'd heard it, too. Amazing how Miss O' and I could pick out a single sour note. She started again, like a policeman directing traffic. The music swelled, jerked, sank and swelled again.

Suddenly, her arms fell limp at her sides. "Awful, sim-m-mply aw-w-wful," she bellowed. We repeated and repeated the section for what seemed like hours. Finally, we finished the piece.

Our teacher collapsed in a heap on her stool. "Let's take a break."

At the water fountain, Miss O' soaked her handkerchief and swabbed her face, tipping her wig crooked. I chuckled to myself. Too bad Skip wasn't here to see it. I stepped up and sucked in some water. Dribbles ran down my chin.

"Hope you play violin better than you drink water." Marcy leaned forward and pulled her long red hair out of the way before taking a sip. "Good thing Miss O' has me in her orchestra."

I glared at her, rolling my shoulder up to dry my chin.

Miss O' called us to return to our seats.

Marcy sat down, fanning her face with the sheet music, and waited. "Good day for a dip at the swimming hole."

I stared at her. "You've been there?"

"Oh sure!"

"Did anyone see you?"

"Nah, I snuck through the woods. Gotta enjoy it before things change." She raised her eyebrows. "They're cutting up the oak, you know."

I had to admit that Marcy had guts. I watched her as she rearranged her music. Her thick red eyelashes were at least an inch long and they touched her cheekbone when she blinked.

"*Star-Spangled Banner* is next," called Miss O'. "Elliot, ready for your solo? Elliot!"

I jumped, feeling my face heat up.

Marcy tapped my knee with her bow. "Don't miss any notes, Champ!"

So what if her eyelashes were an inch long, she'd still be a pain.

The teacher swept her arms upward and the music flowed.

The more I concentrated on hitting the right notes, the sweatier my hands became. The moment approached. I shifted my hand to third position to start my solo. I played the first note— a sour one. I tried to correct my intonation, but missed another note, and another until my fingers were hopelessly tangled.

Tap! Tap! Tap! Miss O' stopped the orchestra. She frowned. "Young man, what was *that?*"

A shiver zinged up my spine. "Uh...I'm sorry, Miss O'Looney. It's really hot in here."

A snarky whisper came from you-know-who. "Wish I could play like that."

Looking exasperated, Miss O' directed the musicians to begin again. I wiped my wet palms on my cargo shorts.

This time I forgot about Marcy, and myself too. My fingers glided over the strings, hitting every single note. The long smooth strokes of my bow made sweet music as the other instruments joined me. With a final swoop of Miss O's baton, we ended together. I was awesome. Not one mistake. Take *that* Marcy!

Deadman's Pocket

After a moment of silence, Marcy started the applause, whistling through her teeth. Miss O' plopped on her stool and looked pleased.

We practiced one last piece before rehearsal ended. As everyone clamored to pack up, the teacher shouted instructions for Saturday's rehearsal. The cafeteria emptied in minutes, except Miss O' and me.

Not eager to ask Miss O' about missing a rehearsal, I took my time gently wiping away the rosin dust under the strings. With the bow and violin nestled in their velvet-lined pockets, I snapped the latches closed.

"Mr. Wermann!" Miss O' called from the door, tapping her foot. "What is taking you so long? I have a private lesson across town in twenty minutes."

I hurried over to her. "Miss O', I wondered, I mean, I need to..."

"What?" asked Miss O', sighing impatiently.

"I need to be excused from rehearsal this Saturday."

Her face dropped, looking a bit pale. "Why? Is anything wrong?"

"It's just that I have an important appointment. But I'd be back for the final Saturday rehearsal, though."

"Elliot, you're the concertmaster, the leader of the orchestra. What will the other students think if you're not here?" She paused and looked at me as if she smelled something fishy. "Maybe you don't want the solo?"

"O' course, I do. I know it backwards, forwards and sideways."

"Today made me doubt that."

"I just messed up a little today, that's all. "

"Mistakes are inevitable."

Oh good, she was going to let it pass.

"Then again, I suppose Marcy Bettencourt could substitute. She's been practicing the solo and she's been asking...."

Marcy tried to steal my solo away from me? What a sneak! "Please, Miss O', I want the solo!"

"Then be here on Saturday."

8
Two Big Dilemmas

I took the long route home, pedaling so slowly I could hardly steer. I wasn't eager to see anyone, especially Skip. He'd bug me to go to the tryouts even if it meant missing the rehearsal. To do both, I needed a plan, and quick.

The old wooden planks of the big red Taftsville covered bridge clattered under my tires. I always feared a board would crack and I'd drop like lead into the dark river below, drowning my violin, my bike and me. I held my breath as I sped up. Crossing safely, I peeled a right turn off the bridge, then down the steep hillside. Old River Road was above on my left; the Ottauquechee River was twelve feet below on my right. I picked up the pace. The path cut through thickets of donkey rhubarb weeds and shady maple trees. For a few minutes I pedaled, raising plenty of dust, turning my black bike to grey. An occasional branch whipped me in the face. I didn't care. I loved weaving through the narrow spaces between the trees. With my heart racing, I skidded to a halt.

A woodpecker hammered a tree trunk nearby. A squirrel skittered through a clump of bushes.

Water lapped at the bank. I stood directly across the river from the swimming hole. There lay the rotting oak. I was afraid to blink and see the accident again.

Two figures moved on the rock ledge. I propped up my bike, set down my violin, and scrambled up the hillside for a better view across the river. Jace and Duke! I checked my cell phone. Two o'clock. Dad was at work and Mom must have gone shopping. Bluish smoke clouds billowed over their heads. This was the second time I'd seen Jace smoking with Duke. First time was last year under the bleachers at Ipes Park.

Suddenly, Duke pointed at me. "Hey! Hey!"

I raced down the hill, arms flailing for balance, almost tripping headfirst. Grabbing my violin, I sped away. The path ended at Tibbetts Wick Road, which led toward home.

When I got home Skip was sitting on my front lawn under our shady elm, sipping Gatorade. He waved a hello.

I hung up my bike in the garage as usual and dusted off my violin case. Then I guzzled water from the garden hose before I sat down next to him.

Skip belched and said, "Did you ask her?"

Instead of answering, I told him about Miss O's wig slipping over her forehead at the water fountain. He laughed and rolled around in the grass. When he caught his breath, Skip propped himself on one elbow and repeated. "So, did you ask her?"

Stalling for time, I slapped dust off my sneakers.

"Well?" asked Skip.

"She said no."

Skip sprang to a sitting position. "That sucks. What did you say, exactly?"

The whole story spilled out. How Marcy threw me off. How I got the jitters. How Miss O' almost took away my solo. How I'd seen my brother and Duke smoking on the rock ledge a minute ago, even though Jace is grounded.

"Yeah, well, you and I are still on for Saturday," said Skip.

"But my rehearsal."

"You promised to do the tryouts with me!"

"It's a solo! I can't bail."

"Aw, come on!"

I knew he wouldn't give up. I racked my brain for a way to get out of rehearsal. "I've got it!" The Star Wars theme song blared in my head. "It'll be perfect."

"Awesome!" said Skip. "Tell me!"

I stood up. "Not now, later."

"No fair. I'll—"

A loud commotion came from Skip's house. His mother's shrill voice pierced the air, followed by cupboard slamming. We raced to his back door leading into the kitchen.

Shirley Manis

There was his three-year-old sister Marianna sitting on the kitchen floor. Her white T-shirt and denim overalls covered with egg yolks.

"Will you look at this mess!" exclaimed Skip's mother, wiping Marianna's face and hands with a wet towel.

"Where baby chickies, Ma ma?" cried Marianna, showing her hands with broken eggshells stuck to her fingers.

"Marianna, no baby chicks in the eggs," said her mother.

Skip rolled his eyes and yanked me back outside. "Let's get out of here before she makes me help clean up!"

"Michael, come here," called Skip's mom.

Too late.

He punched the air then waved me a goodbye. "Remember, you've only got tomorrow and Friday to put your perfect plan into action."

How could I forget?

9
The Comic Book

Mom flung open my bedroom door without knocking. She hummed a tune as she walked to the window and raised the blinds. "Time to get up! You've slept long enough."

I groaned and rubbed my eyes. Summertime was for sleeping in.

"Today, it's the attic," said Mom with too much cheerfulness. She rummaged through the piles of clothes on my floor, collecting a load of laundry. "We'll sort through the cedar chest and donate the most usable things to Goodwill."

"Aw, do I have to?" I yawned. All night I'd tossed and turned trying to figure out a plan to get to the tryouts. All I could come up with was to change the time. I'd have to convince Jace to do that. But why would he? He was already fuming because I got him grounded. I had to think harder. I couldn't care less about the dumb attic.

"Yes, you have to." Mom stopped and sniffed a pair of cargo shorts. She must have decided they were clean enough and hung them up on my wall hook. "After that, you can clean up the rest of this mess." Except for shoving my chair under my desk and straightening my signed photo of violinist Itzhak Perlman, she didn't touch anything in my music corner. "We'd better get moving. The collection truck will be here this afternoon. You want to help the poor, don't you?"

Mom's favorite guilt trip. She said needy kids don't have enough clothing to wear or toys to play with. It was good to be generous toward less fortunate people. Okay, so giving to the poor anytime was a great idea, but why today?

I swung my feet to the floor and slouched on the edge of my bed. "Where's Jace? Why don't you recruit him?"

"Your dad dropped your brother off at Ipes Park on his way to Boston."

I flopped back on the bed. "How come Jace gets to play?"

Mom turned to me, holding the bundle of clothes she'd gathered. My dirty socks dangled over her arm. "He's helping Mr. Pazaropoulos pull weeds and plant flowers for the 4th of July festivities."

I chuckled to myself, picturing Jace on his hands and knees, listening to Mr. P's endless stories about his Greek mountain village. "When's Dad coming back?"

"Saturday at suppertime – he's taking Grandma Carol to her doctor appointments."

I faked another yawn and stretched my arms over my head, hoping she'd leave me alone.

"Your juice and cereal are on the kitchen table," Mom called back as she headed downstairs.

After breakfast, I clomped up the creaky attic steps behind Mom. The air was hot and stuffy. She pulled the string on the only light bulb, which didn't throw much light. Every time she shifted boxes, I coughed from the dust.

"Here it is," said Mom, out of breath. She knelt down in front of her old chest, pressed its button latch and lifted the dusty lid. The smell of cedar wood mixed with mothballs made me gag. Mom dug inside, mumbling to herself. She pulled out the yellow hospital blanket I was wrapped in after I was born and went all gooey-eyed. Then she found Jace's first Christmas flannel sleeper and she hugged that, too. My day was slipping away while she daydreamed.

I sighed, looking for a place to sit. My little baby blue stool was in the corner. I grabbed it and screamed. "Ouch!"

Mom dropped the clothes in the chest. "What's wrong?"

"I got a splinter!" I squeezed the fingertips of my bow hand really hard to make them turn extra deep red.

"Let's get it out right now." Mom slammed the chest shut and we rushed down to the bathroom.

She examined my finger furiously, searching for the sliver of wood. I faked cries of pain.

"Honey, I don't see anything. I really don't."

"Maybe it fell out."

She dropped my hand and peered at me. "Splinters don't just fall out."

Capster's voice echoed up the stairwell from the front door. "Hey, Elliot! You home?"

"Yeah!" I yelled so loud that Mom winced.

"There's soccer games at Ipes Park. Tell Skip and come on."

I gave Mom a pitiful *puppy-dog look*.

She sighed. "Oh, go on. Never mind the attic."

I kissed her cheek. "Thanks, Mom!" Then I shouted to Capster, "Coming! Be right there!"

My idea to ask Jace for a time change could wait. He was tied up with Mr. P anyway. I bounded down the stairs.

Mom called from the bathroom. "Have fun!"

"I will!"

Skip and I hopped on our bikes. Halfway to Ipes, he veered toward the pharmacy.

"Where are you going?" I shouted at him.

"I've been saving my allowance for a new pair of shades," said Skip. "The latest ones should have arrived at Curry's Pharmacy by now."

We locked our bikes behind the brick building.

Our neighborhood drugstore sold more than laxatives and prescriptions, like magazines, candy, plastic model car kits, live goldfish and little bottles of perfume I buy for Mom every Christmas. Skip pulled open the door and we stepped inside. The cool air smelled of sugar and disinfectants.

Passing the gurgling fish tank, Skip bonked the surface and the little creatures darted inside their underwater castles.

The sunglasses were near the back wall. Skip spun the turnstile, trying on pair after pair. "Just look at these beauties!"

I shifted from leg to leg, waiting.

"How 'bout these?" asked Skip.

The dark lenses bulged over his cheesy smile and made him look like an insect. "Good enough," I said.

"Okay, let's go," said Skip.

As we went to pay, I put my arm out across his chest and whispered, "Uh-oh." Marcy had stepped up to the cash register. Mr. Curry scanned her items – a little notebook, a Sharpie and pack of chewing gum – and announced her total. She spotted us and grinned. "Well, if it isn't the violin superstar! Shouldn't you be practicing?"

"Already did,"

"Getting ready for the games, I suppose?" asked Marcy, not looking up as she searched her coin purse.

"What games?" Was she talking about soccer or tryouts?

"You know, over at Ipes right now," said Marcy as she spun around and headed to the door. "Ta, ta."

While Skip paid for his shades, I went to the magazine aisle. I thumbed through an action comic book.

"Buy a magazine or get moving," scolded Mr. Curry. His scowling face turned into a smile when his next customer stepped up.

Outside, the hot, humid air blasted us. Wouldn't you know it, Duke walked up at that same moment. "Who you spying on today, Viddle-man?" He jostled me out of his way and punched me in the arm before he went inside.

Skip turned to me. "What's with him?"

I shrugged. "Maybe he's mad I spotted him on the rock ledge with Jace."

Suddenly, Duke burst out the door. He ran full-speed and jammed a magazine into my chest as he passed me.

"What's that for?" asked Skip.

I frowned. It was the same comic book I'd just looked at.

"Happy Birthday, Waddle-man," said Duke as he kept on running. He disappeared around the corner of the building.

Did Duke like me now or something?

Out of the corner of my eye, a red-faced Mr. Curry charged out the door toward us.

Without thinking, I stuffed the comic book down the back of my cargo shorts and stood tall.

"Did you see that kid with anything?" asked Mr. Curry, panting.

"No sir." I replied, pushing out my belly to keep my shorts tight at the waist.

Skip's jaw dropped.

"Damn teenager is always here stealing something. Don't you boys pick up his bad ways." The pharmacist went inside, shaking his head.

I let out a big sigh of relief. The comic book sank deeper into my shorts.

"What are you thinking?" asked Skip. "Give it back!"

I pulled out the comic book. "Nope, not a chance. It could help me."

"Oh yeah, how? If you're caught with that comic book, you'll be in trouble, not Duke," said Skip, "and, your dad will freak."

"I know. But if I don't get Duke into trouble, even though he's guilty, then Jace might be reasonable and help me with my plan."

"You promised to tell me about your perfect plan," said Skip as he put on his new shades. "Whatever it is, I sure hope it works."

10

Perfect Plan Revealed

As I rounded the building, I rammed into Duke, and Skip crashed into me. The comic book popped out of my hand. Duke caught it mid-air.

"Hey," said Duke with a menacing look, riffling the pages. "Look what you stole! Yo, Mr. Cur-rry—,"

"Hey, you can't hang that on me."

Duke held the comic book under my nose and twisted the flimsy pages until they tore, then tossed the mangled mess into the bushes along the building. "I can do anything I want," sneered Duke. "Just so you know, I'm running RBC now."

I gulped.

"You're in charge?" asked Skip, wide-eyed. "What happened to Jace?"

"None of your business," smirked Duke.

Why would Jace give up his club? If Duke was the new leader, that really changed everything.

That was my perfect plan, to get the start time of the tryouts changed to three o'clock. Then I could go to my orchestra rehearsal at one o'clock and still make it to the tryouts. Perfect. But now, I'll have to ask Duke to change the tryout time. This is not good.

"Give me what I want and I won't tell Mr. Curry you stole the comic book," I said before my knees started to cave."

Duke chuckled. "Really now? What would that be, little Weary-man?"

I blurted as fast as I could, "Change the tryout time to three o'clock."

Skip's eyes grew wide.

"In your dreams."

"I'm serious. You're the leader. You make the rules. Why not?"

"Let...me...see." Duke tapped his chin with his index finger, acting like he was thinking.

"Well?" I winked at Skip who now understood that a time change for the tryouts was my perfect plan.

Duke exploded in laughter, spraying me with his stinking spit. "No favors for thieves, Worm-man. As advertised, the fun begins at one o'clock."

I wiped the slime off my face. "Then I'll snitch about your smoking."

"So what? Smoking's no crime."

"But using pot is." That just fell out of my mouth. "I'll call the cops!"

Duke froze and glared at me.

Sweat rolled down my forehead.

The bully leaped at me, grabbed my throat and pushed me up against the brick building until we were nose-to-nose. Suddenly, his knife flashed in my face. "Say anything, twit and I'll fix your neck." His tight hold and gross breath choked me.

"Take it easy," said Skip, reaching to pull Duke's hand off me.

"Stay out of this," snarled Duke.

My heart banged in my chest as I hung in his grip.

Skip dropped his hands.

I kept on going. "Don't forget," I croaked. "You spray painted the principal's mailbox, too." I was dying for some air.

Duke tightened his grasp, growled something then slowly released me. "Deal. The new time is three o'clock. Keep your fat trap shut or you'll be playing your squeak box with two less fingers." Duke licked the knife before he pocketed it, then took off.

I coughed, bent over, hands on my knees.

Skip slapped me on the back. "Awesome! Way to go, dude!"

"You heard what he said, didn't you?' I said rubbing my neck.

"Sure did. I'm your witness," Skip said.

"Now, there's no time conflict with my rehearsal and the tryouts!"

"Yep, but how'd you find out about the pot?" asked Skip.

"I made it up."

Skip's jaw dropped. "You lied?"

"Call it a good guess and it worked, didn't it?" I said, breathing a lot better.

"You lied about the mailbox, too?" asked Skip.

"No. I knew Jace climbed out his window that night to meet Duke."

"You didn't actually see him spray paint the principal's mailbox, did you?"

"Didn't have to. That was another guess. I know the guys. I live with one."

Skip unwrapped a piece of bubble gum and popped it into his mouth, then jerked his head in the direction of Ipes Park. "Come on, we're late, Wolf-man!"

I smiled. "Wermann. My name is Wermann.

I was pumped. We raced on our bikes. Running every stop sign, I held the lead. Skip and I cruised through the park gates past rows and rows of freshly planted red, white and blue flowers. Jace had been busy.

Marcy and her friends were jumping double ropes on the asphalt, chanting rhymes. Capster, Reggie and boys from all over town huddled near the coach, who was shouting instructions.

Skip and I elbowed through the crowd to where Capster stood. "You're late. What kept you?"

"So much time has elapsed," said Reggie, adjusting the elastic head strap he used to hold his glasses on tight.

Shirley Manis

The coach put my friends on the same team and told Skip to toss his bubblegum. During the team rotations, Skip and I spread the news of Duke's takeover and the three o'clock time change.

The games lasted until dusk and I cheered until I lost my voice. Capster led the team to a five-point victory. Lots of high-fives and chest bumping.

Skip and I pedaled home. I watched our dim shadows grow and shrink as we passed under streetlights. He pulled into his driveway and waved goodbye.

I hung up my bike in the garage as usual and went inside. "I'm home!" No one answered. No sign of Jace either. In the utility room, six humongous shopping bags overflowed with clothes and toys. The collection truck must not have showed up. I ignored my usual urge to search and rescue some favorite things. It was Mom's book club night. She left a note on the kitchen whiteboard telling Jace and me to fix ourselves something to eat.

I opened the freezer and found a pizza to cook in the microwave. I guzzled glasses of cold water until my stomach cramped. I took the last Dr. Pepper and marched upstairs to eat in my room.

I sat on the floor, sinking my teeth into my favorite pepperoni and cheese and sucked down the soda. After I licked the pizza tray clean and crushed the empty can, I removed all signs that I'd disobeyed a house rule – no food in bedrooms. I don't know why I bothered. My room still looked like a tornado passed through it.

I tuned my violin and whipped through my practice exercises and solo without any errors. Saturday's rehearsal would be a piece of cake. I played until ten o'clock then put everything away. Where were Jace and Mom? Dad was still not home from Grandma Carol's.

The quiet house reminded me of the afternoon I'd spent alone on the day of Billy's funeral. I missed Billy. He would have been stoked about how I stood up to Duke today. I crawled into bed and rolled up in my sheet like a pig-in-a-blanket.

I, Elliot Wermann, was not going to be a loser.

11

Spying

Next thing I knew it was morning. Somebody grabbed my heels and dragged me out from under the sheets onto the floor. I landed on my tailbone. "Ow!"

"You moron," Jace hissed through his teeth.

I rubbed my butt and scuttled back up onto my bed. "What?"

Jace rolled up the sheet and tossed it into my face. "You're a thief and a snitch!" His blue eyes got real wide. Scary wide. "And dumber than a rock, too."

"What are you talking about?"

"Duke said you threatened to tell old man Curry that he stole a comic book."

"He did steal the comic, then he was going to blame it on me!"

"That's not how I heard it."

"Ask Skip, my witness. He was there."

"He'll just lie for you."

I'd never seen Jace's face and neck so red.

"And the weed," said Jace, moving closer.

"What about it?"

"How'd you know?" asked Jace.

So it was true. "I'm not dumb," I said. "I saw you and Duke smoking on the rock ledge."

"If you know what's good for you, you'll keep your mouth shut. I don't need any more hassles." Jace pointed his finger at me. "Well?"

"I won't say a word to anybody 'cuz I asked Duke to change the tryout time to three o'clock."

Jace looked puzzled. "How could he?" His face turned white. "It's my club. I make the rules."

So Duke did not have Jace's permission to take over RBC. I shifted on the bed, and my tailbone ached with pain. "Then...you're the one to ask."

"You got that right, Squeaky. RBC is my idea, my club." Jace puffed up his chest and stood firm. "And my time for tryouts is at one o'clock, got it?"

"But everybody at the soccer games already found out that Duke changed the time to three o'clock."

"Whose side you on?"

"My own. Hey, I'm not going down for Duke's crimes. Nobody has to find out about the stolen comic book or the weed because Duke did as I wanted and changed the time for me. Now I can get to my rehearsal." Jace took a step closer. But I couldn't stop. "You're grounded on Saturday. If you try to change the time back to one o'clock, I'll tell Dad about your smoking." I folded my arms across my chest in a huff.

I'd seen that look in his eyes before. He wanted to take a punch at me. I raised my arm, guarding against a swing.

"You scummy rat!" shouted Jace. "Just wait and—"

"Jason! Elliot! Stop that arguing," called Mom from downstairs. "Jason, get down here now. Mr. Pazaropoulos is here to take you to Ipes Park."

Jace sneered at me.

"Hurry! He's waiting," said Mom more impatiently.

"Yeah, I'm coming," Jace started toward the door.

I crawled to the edge of my bed. "By the way, where were you so late last night?"

Jace stopped cold, turned and looked at me. "Like I'm ever going to tell you anything, so you can twist it into a lie?"

"I told you! I'm not lying! The comic book, the takeover, the smoking-- they're all facts!"

"Good luck proving it." Jace turned on his heel, walked out, and slammed the door hard enough to rattle my window. He hated me and it was mutual.

I yelled at the closed door. "Jerk!"

"Same to you, Squeaky," shouted Jace as he thundered down the stairs.

My butt still hurt. I got off the bed, slowly. I held my breath until I heard the crash of the front door screen. At least Jace was out of my sight for the day.

I picked up my violin and practiced for an hour and a half straight. Mom knocked on my door and peeked in. "Skip's out front."

"Who?" I smiled to myself.

"You know, your best friend," said Mom. "I'm taking those donations to Goodwill. Go have some fun."

I put away my instrument and hurried downstairs. Skip was waiting on the front porch steps.

"Hey," said Skip. "Tomorrow's the big day."

I sat down gingerly next to him.

"What's wrong?" asked Skip. "Aren't you excited?"

"Jace and I had a major blow up this morning."

"About?"

"Jace still thinks he's the RBC leader and wants the tryouts to stay at one o'clock."

"But everyone's going at three o'clock," said Skip.

"I know," I said. "Let's get out of here. A walk might clear my brain."

"Okay."

We ended up at Ipes Park. Mr P and Jace were nowhere around.

"Wanna go to the rock ledge?" asked Skip, waiting. "Let's scope out the place again before the tryouts."

I paused. The voice in my head yelled I'd be breaking Dad's order by going to the swimming hole.

"Something wrong?" asked Skip.

I shook my head and gave a thumb up. We scurried to the new chain link fence.

"Ready?"

"Ready."

We dropped to our knees and dug through the loose dirt near one of the metal posts. He shimmied under first. At the end of the path, we eased through the bushes onto the rock ledge. When we sat, I shifted around until my butt stopped hurting. We didn't say anything for a while, soaking up the rays and listening to the gentle sound of rushing water.

"There it is," I said, staring. "Deadman's Pocket."

"Hey, that's the first time you've called it Deadman's Pocket," said Skip.

"Yeah, because it's true. Billy is a dead man now."

Suddenly, Duke's voice rang out below us on the bank. Skip and I sprawled out onto our stomachs and peered over the edge. I heard other voices but I couldn't see anybody else. Then, Biff and Mudge moved into view. What were Duke and his buddies doing?

"Over here," yelled Duke, pointing upward. "I got the rope and that tree limb looks sturdy enough and hangs over the water."

Biff and Mudge both agreed.

"I'll double-check," said Duke, removing his shoes, he quickly climbed up the huge maple tree.

"What do you think they're up to?" I whispered.

Skip shrugged.

Duke reached the limb. He wrapped a rope around the limb, tied knots over and over again, then pounded nails through the rope into the limb.

"No kidding. It's a rope swing," said Skip.

"Let's test it." Duke gave a final whack with his hammer, so the rope wouldn't shift or unravel. Then he coiled up the rope and draped it one last time over the limb.

Biff and Mudge began to climb the tree to take their turn.

"Wait, wait," said Duke. "The limb can't hold all of us up here. One at a time. I'll go first."

Duke looped the free end of the rope around his wrist, bent his knees and pushed off. He sailed far out over the swimming hole. At the moment Duke started to swing back, he let go. He had a split second of hang time before he dropped, feet first, clothes and all. He landed with a huge splash and stayed under for what seemed like minutes. Finally, Duke broke through the surface, mouth open wide, and gasping. He swam over to the boys on the bank.

"Hit bottom?" asked Biff.

"Yeah," said Duke, catching his breath.

"Cool!" said Mudge.

"Must be ten, maybe twelve feet deep! Really mucky down there," said Duke. "I got stuck when I pushed to come back up. Almost ran out of air. Jace dreamed up this wicked test and I put up the rope just like Jace wanted it done. Tons more dangerous than the log."

The boys exchanged fist bumps.

Skip turned and stared at me.

I swallowed hard. What came up burned my throat.

12

The Phone Call

Skip and I watched as Duke, Mudge and Biff took turns on the rope swing. We were too curious to leave. Jumping from a high limb in the maple tree sent chills down my spine.

After a few swings, they complained the coarse rope made burns on their wrists. I worried about my hands, getting rope burns or blisters would make it hard to play my solo. I could tell Skip couldn't wait to have his turn tomorrow.

The rock ledge was getting hot. We crawled back through the bushes, up the path and under the fence. Duke had no clue we'd discovered the new test for tomorrow.

"I could go for a cold drink," I said.

"Me, too," said Skip.

At 7-Eleven, we chose our slushies, root beer for me and bubblegum for Skip. We fished around in our pockets and dumped our coins on the counter. We were short a quarter.

The bells on the door jingled. Duke strolled in and walked straight to the refrigerated cases along the back wall.

"Come on, you need another quarter," said the clerk, rapping his knuckles on the counter next to our drinks. "Pay up or go thirsty."

Skip and I double-checked for more money.

Duke stepped up, pushing me out of his way. He put a cold soda and a bag of chips on the counter. Then Duke and the clerk did some kind of secret handshake. Finger grips, twists and a final high five.

"You rule," said the clerk.

"What's going on here?" Duke eyed the coins on the counter. "Do my friends have a problem?"

I wasn't Duke's friend and never would be.

"Yep," said the clerk. "They're short a quarter for these drinks."

"Hang on." Duke dug a quarter out of his pocket and flipped it into the air. It landed, spinning next to all the other coins. "There ya go!"

When the coin settled down the clerk swept the money off the counter and into the cash register. Skip reached for our sweating drink cups.

"Thanks," I said, cracking a small smile.

"Tomorrow," said Duke as he turned away and left.

"He didn't pay," I said to the clerk.

The clerk said seriously, "I'll collect later."

Outside we found an empty bus stop bench.

"Can you believe that?" asked Skip. "Duke took the soda and chips, and the clerk just let him have them."

"Yeah, he's bad news. No wonder Jace always gets into trouble with him. But we should look on the bright side. He gave us the quarter we needed."

Skip spit out his straw. "But he shoulda paid for his stuff."

"The clerk said he'd collect later." I swallowed a big gulp. " Who knows? Maybe he's selling dope to Duke?"

Skip rubbed the sweaty cup against his arm to cool off. "And, I don't want to find out."

"Me neither."

While we finished our drinks, Skip called out the makes and models of the cars zooming by. Skip knew them all. O' course, I could name more symphonies than he could. Our conversation drifted around to Billy and how we missed him. I tossed my empty plastic cup and paper straw in the recycle bin and so did Skip. "I'd better be heading home," I said.

"Me, too," said Skip. "Tomorrow will be awesome. We'll become River Boys. Wait and see."

"First, I'll go to rehearsal, then we'll have a wild time!"

As we walked, the afternoon breeze smelled of grilling burgers, which made me hungry. For the first time in a long time, I felt happy, ready to take on the world. I waved goodbye to Skip.

I stepped into the kitchen. The phone was ringing.

"Would you get that?" called Mom from somewhere in the house.

"Sure!" I answered the phone and said, "Hello, Wermann residence."

"Elliot?" said a woman's voice.

"Speaking."

"This is Miss O'Looney."

13
How to Choose?

I'd never spoken to a teacher on the phone. Nothing came out of my mouth.

"Hello? Hello? Is anyone there?"

"Yes, Miss O'Looney. It's me, Elliot."

"Just the person I wanted to talk to. Elliot, I have to change tomorrow's rehearsal to three o'clock. The electricians will be installing energy-saving lights and they won't finish until two o'clock."

"But, I–"

"I'm sure you'll make whatever arrangements are necessary about that important appointment of yours so you can be there on time."

I didn't say a word.

"Elliot, are you there?"

"Yes, Miss O'Looney," I spoke softly. "I heard."

"Tomorrow then. Good-bye." She hung up.

I slammed the phone down.

"Who was it?" asked Mom coming into the kitchen.

"Wrong number," I said, staring at the phone.

"I was hoping it was your father telling us when he'd be coming home from Grandma

Carol's." She paused and reached for my forehead. "You don't look well."

I brushed her hand away. "I'm okay." I ran to my room, flung myself onto the bed and pounded the pillow. My life sucked. How could I be a River Boy now? What was I going to do? I rolled over on my back and called Skip.

"You'll never guess what Miss O' just did," I said.

"I give. What?" asked Skip.

"She moved rehearsal to three o'clock, same time as the tryouts. She didn't give me a chance to remind her about my important appointment."

"What important appointment?" asked Skip.

"The tryouts, of course, but I never told her exactly what the appointment was. I just needed to tell her something she'd believe. And she did."

"Dude, you're screwed."

"Tell me something I don't know."

"So, now what?" asked Skip.

"I'm thinking," I said, chewing my lip.

"Remember, you promised to go. Can't back out on me now."

"I know, I know. And then there's Marcy wanting my solo. I don't have any ideas right now."

"Well, call me when you figure something out."

I hung up. Skip was no help. My stomach felt like someone grabbed it and twisted it into a knot.

I heard Jace tromp up the stairs. Minutes later, his stereo blasted Hip-Hop. The rhythms gave me a headache. He'd never lower the volume if I complained. After our fight this morning, he wouldn't do anything for me. He hated me as much as I hated him.

I needed to escape the racket and followed the aroma of a baking pie to the kitchen.

Mom was chopping vegetables. "Hi honey."

I dragged out a chair from under the table, sat down and cradled my head in my hands.

"Something on your mind?" asked Mom.

I wanted to tell her everything right then so she could help me decide what to do about the new mess Miss O' just created for me. Mom could always straighten things out. But if I spilled my guts, I'd ruin it for all my friends, and be in even more trouble for deliberately disobeying Dad. I needed to talk to someone.

"Remember that call earlier?"

"Yes."

"It was really Miss O'Looney."

Mom stopped chopping and looked sideways at me. "And—what did she want?"

"Saturday's rehearsal was changed to three o'clock."

"Is that a problem?" asked Mom.

"Kinda."

"Why?"

I was ready to tell her. "Well, all the guys–"

Ping! The timer went off.

Mom put on her oven mitts, pulled out a golden-crusted blueberry pie and set it on a rack to cool. "You were saying?"

I drooled. "Ah, nothing important. Can I have some?" A piece of pie could take my mind off my troubles.

"You'll have to wait. This is for dessert," said Mom. "By the way, I've told the women in the Charity League about your solo".

"Aw, why'd you do that?" She always bragged about me.

"Because I'm so proud of you. That's why." She dumped a can of tomatoes into the pot on the stove and stirred in the vegetables. "So is your father."

"Dad?" Proud of me? All I ever got from him was criticism.

"You know, your father loves you." She covered the pot.

"Says who?" I asked.

"Me. I know he doesn't always show it, but he loves both of you boys."

"Then how come he hangs out with Jace so much and doesn't with me? He never asks about my violin."

"He doesn't understand it," said Mom. "You're the most musical person in our family. Jason happens to be more athletic is all, like your father."

Mom raised an eyebrow. "Did you know your brother is jealous of you?"

Yeah, right.

"Jason told me he'd never be as good at playing an instrument as you," said Mom. "You both have your strengths: yours is music, Jason has sports. Both terrific qualities, I must say!"

Then my mind reeled again with what was I going to do about the tryouts? I decided to chance it with her. "Can I ask you a question?"

"Sure, anything."

"What if a friend of mine had two activities at the same time, both were really important, but he could only do one? How does he choose?" I asked.

She lifted the lid of her simmering pot and looked down inside as if the answer were in there. "I'd make two lists with all the reasons I'd do each activity. The list with the most good reasons would win."

"But what if both lists have the same number of wins?"

"Oh, then I'd simply do the one that makes me the happiest," said Mom.

She was a modern marvel. A genius! "Thanks, Mom." I stood to leave.

Shirley Manis

"That's all?" Her eyebrows disappeared under her bangs.

I was gone in a flash. In my room, I grabbed a pencil and a pad of paper and sat down by the open window. I made two columns—one for the tryouts and one for the rehearsal. I started with the rehearsal list:

1) I'd play my violin.
2) I'd get to play my solo.
3) I'd still be the concertmaster.
4) Miss O' and my parents would be proud of me.
5) I'd be far away from Deadman's Pocket, and obeying Dad's orders.

On the other hand, if I went to RBC tryouts:

1) I'd be honoring Billy.
2) I'd be with all friends.
3) Skip would be happy.
4) I wouldn't be called a loser.
5) I could prove to Jace that I had guts and was worthy of being in his club.

I looked at my paper. Both had the same number of reasons. Mom had said to choose the one that made me the happiest. That was easy, the rehearsal.

Then Billy popped into my head again. He'd died playing at the swimming hole because of me. Deep down, I was afraid to go back to

Deadman's Pocket, no matter what Skip said, so I was okay when Dad banned me from that place. But if I didn't return to the swimming hole and compete for the River Boys Club, I'd be frightened of Deadman's Pocket for the rest of my life and who knows what else. If I really wanted to be happy, first I needed to conquer my fear. That was it. I couldn't change my mind. I'd just have to face whatever punishment Dad had for me and I didn't care how bad it was.

    Tomorrow was Saturday and I had to become a River Boy, no matter what.

14
Who is the Leader?

Mom tapped on my bedroom door and peeked in. "I can't stand the heat anymore. I'm going to the mall."

"Cool."

"I certainly hope it will be." She swiped sweat from her forehead.

I checked my clock. It was just after two. "When will you be back?"

"Probably around five. Your father won't be home till seven so I have a few hours to myself." She winked, pulled the door shut.

Could it be true? I couldn't have planned this Saturday better if I'd tried.

The coast was clear for Deadman's Pocket. I had chosen and didn't care that I would miss rehearsal.

I texted Skip. "You ready?"

He replied. "Now or never."

We biked to the fence, crawled under and ran down the path to the rock ledge.

Once there, I heard voices, but nothing like the usual yelling and hollering. We stripped to our swim trunks and tossed our clothes under the bushes. Capster and Reggie treaded water below.

Deadman's Pocket

Biff and Mudge were hanging out around on the log. Duke hadn't arrived yet.

Skip and I called out, "Geronimo!" and charged off the rock ledge.

When we surfaced, Capster and Reggie swam over.

"Awesome! More contestants," said Reggie wiping the lenses of his water goggles.

"What happened to your rehearsal?" said Capster.

"I didn't make the cut." I laughed.

"Lo-o-oser!" Capster teased with a smile.

Biff and Mudge joined us. A mini water fight broke out.

"Isn't it time to start the fun?" asked Biff a few minutes later.

"Yeah, but where's Duke?" Mudge blinked hard to get water out of his eyes.

"Heads up!" bellowed Duke, from the rock ledge above us. "Your leader is here!" He arched high and dove into our circle. The splash sent choppy waves in every direction, driving water up my nose. I snorted.

Duke surfaced at least fifteen feet away and spouted like a whale.

"Come on, guys" said Duke. He swam over and climbed up onto the bank.

We joined him.

"Today, there will be three tests. First test, you have to carry one of these into the water," said

Duke, pointing at the pile of large rocks he'd collected, "and, stay under for at least ten seconds. You get three tries."

The smooth, moss-covered limestone rocks looked heavy and were as big as volleyballs!

"What if you don't accomplish it in three tries?" asked Reggie.

"You're out," said Duke.

"Just like that?" asked Reggie.

"Are you deaf?"

I could tell Reggie was nervous because he backed up and fidgeted with the drawstrings on his swim trunks.

"What are the other two tests?" asked Capster.

"You'll find out soon enough," said Duke.

Skip glanced at me and smiled. We'd seen the wicked rope swing go up. That and the rotting log had to be the other two tests. My armpits felt sticky.

"Let's go! Who's first?" called Duke.

A moment of silence.

"Hey," said Capster, elbowing Reggie's ribs. "You and me."

Reggie stared at the rocks then stepped up with Capster to the pile. They faced the swimming hole and waited.

"Count one-chimpanzee, two-chimpanzee, three-chimpanzee and so on until somebody comes to the surface. I'll count for Capster. Biff, you count for Reggie."

Capster and Reggie each bent down to get a grip on a smooth rock.

Duke stepped aside and raised his arm. "Ready, set—"

"HOLD IT!"

15
Chimpanzees

"What the hell's going on?" said Jace as he pushed through the bushes on the bank. "You guys were supposed to be here at one o'clock."

Skip, Mudge, Biff, and I turned around. Capster and Reggie dropped their rocks.

Jace wore the ugliest scowl I'd ever seen.

"Whatta ya think?" said Duke folding his arms across his chest. "We're having tryouts for the River Boys Club."

As Jace marched toward Duke, we all scrambled out of the way until they were nose-to-nose. I hid behind the group.

"Uh-oh," said Reggie.

"This is going to be interesting," said Skip under his breath.

"This is my club," said Jace.

"Not anymore," said Duke. "I hung the rope swing with Mudge and Biff. Rumors said you were grounded. Somebody had to take over and that somebody is me. What are you doing here anyway?"

"After all my planning for the tests, you think you can just take over? River Boys is my idea, my club. I say when things start."

Duke taunted. "Aren't you supposed to be planting posies today? Hey, did Mr. P follow you here?"

"No and no," Jace puffed up his chest. "I call the shots here, not you! Get it?"

"No, you don't get it!" Duke shoved Jace away with both hands. "These guys showed up at three o'clock because I said so. Who did they listen to? Me. RBC is mine now."

Jace coiled back his arm and slugged Duke in the jaw. The swing knocked Duke flat on his butt. "I just took RBC back. Isn't that right, guys?"

I felt like I should say "Sir, yessir!" Instead, we all huddled closer.

Jace did a double take when he saw me. His eyes grew big. "Squeaky? What are you doing here? Go home!"

Duke struggled to sit up and wiped the blood off his lip.

I half-laughed. "What about you? You're grounded, too. I'm staying."

Jace rubbed his knuckles and glanced over to see where Duke was, then back at me. "Okay, then don't embarrass yourself." He glared at us. "I'm calling the shots now. Are you all in or out?"

I glanced around. My buddies were smiling. We were ready to have some fun.

Jace held out his hand to Duke. "Truce?"

Duke stood and didn't shake hands with Jace, but glowered through the slits of his eyes.

"Maybe." He stomped off and disappeared into the bushes.

"Don't worry, guys. He'll cool off," said Jace, sounding upbeat. "I say we get started." Jace reviewed the tests that he'd planned. He pointed to Capster and Reggie to take your positions. They stepped forward to pick up their smooth rocks again.

"Get ready," shouted Jace. "1-2-3, go!"

They took baby steps with their arms hanging between their legs until they disappeared underwater. Once out of sight, no more bubbles came to the surface. Biff and Mudge kept counting.

"Nine-chimpanzee," called both counters, "ten-chimpanzee!"

Capster and Reggie came up empty-handed, thrashing and gasping for air.

"Hey dudes, where's the rocks?" called Jace.

Capster hollered, "You didn't say we had to bring them back."

"Just kidding," Jace laughed his wicked laugh.

"Woo-hoo! They did it!" called Biff. Cheers broke out as we all exchanged high fives. My friends made it look so easy.

"Next!" shouted Jace.

Biff and Mudge picked up their rocks. Jace counted the chimpanzees, as they both were successful.

"Next contestants!" shouted Jace.

Skip and I went to the pile. I rolled several rocks around looking for a lighter one.

"Stop stalling, get moving," called Jace.

We heaved our rocks off the ground and waddled into the water. My heart was racing from the strain. Why had I chosen that one? I was panting. I sucked in a giant gulp of air.

Water swooshed around me and deadened all sounds, except my thudding heart. The rock hung like a pendulum from my shoulders. As I sank deeper, the rock started to slip. If I dropped the slimy thing, I'd have to do this awful contest a second time. So I tried to tighten my grip. I opened my eyes just as a fish swam straight at my nose. Argh! I dropped the rock and bobbed to the surface.

"Eight-chimpanzee!" shouted Mudge.

"Are you sure?" I asked, coughing out water. "I was down there a long time!"

"Do over. One down, two more," commanded Jace, pointing a thumb at the pile. "Get another one."

I stood near my second rock, rubbing my sore shoulders.

"Eleven-chimpanzee!" shouted Biff. "Skip did it longer!"

Clapping and hooting broke out. Jace motioned to keep the noise down; after all we weren't supposed to even be there. Biff stepped up. He tromped straight into the water and went under before I left the shore. I waddled in again and took a deeper breath. Same pain. Oh no, please hold on. I begged my fingers. Please. Please. OUCH! I bobbed butt first to the surface again.

"Nine-chimpanzee!" shouted Mudge.

My whole body ached.

"Squeaky, just one more chance," warned Jace.

Skip handed me a third rock and whispered. "Here ya go, buddy. You can do this."

Once again, pain. My hands, arms and shoulders felt like they'd explode. Please! Let the time pass. When I couldn't hold it anymore, I dropped the rock and burst to the surface.

"Ten-chimpanzee!" shouted Mudge. "Elliot did it!"

16
Ropes and Somersaults

"Yep," shouted Jace. "Any girl could do it."

I swam to shore. I walked up behind my brother and threw an air punch at his back.

"Chill, Ell," said Skip. "Just concentrate on passing."

He was right. Losing my temper now would only give Jace a chance to humiliate me more.

"What's next?" asked Capster.

"Deadman's swing!" Jace pointed to the rope hanging from a nearby tree.

"Whoa, cool," said Capster.

"Who was the mastermind of that?" asked Reggie.

"Guys, this test is my brainstorm," said Jace.

"Duke brought the rope and nailed it to the limb," shouted Biff. "Duke said he'd done it just like Jace wanted."

Mudge shouted. "Who cares who did what! Bring it on!"

Skip rubbed his hands together. "I've been waiting for this since you guys hung the rope."

I jabbed Skip in the ribs. No one knew we'd spied on them from the rock ledge.

"What do you mean...waiting?" asked Jace, placing a fist on one hip.

"Uh—nothing, really," said Skip.

Jace dropped his arm. "Thought so"

Close call.

"This one's more complicated," said Jace. "Climb the tree, push off, swing out and do a forward somersault."

Somersault? Did he think we were circus acrobats? The rope burns would be bad enough without adding a fall from a tree almost as high as the rock ledge. I clenched my teeth to stop the chattering.

"I can't do a cartwheel let alone a somersault," said Reggie, readjusting his swim goggles.

"I do one-armed cartwheels all the time," said Capster, flexing his biceps. "Somersaults? No prob."

"You are capable of almost anything," said Reggie.

My brother climbed up to the takeoff limb. Jace reeled up the rope and yanked on it, testing to be sure it was secure. He pantomimed the moves. "First, bend your knees. Then shove off and out!"

"Precisely, when do you let go?" asked Reggie nervously.

"Sh-h-h," said Skip. "He's not done."

Jace continued. "When you're far out, you'll hang mid-air for a second or two. Then drop the rope. Tuck forward as if you're going into a dive, but don't. Quickly, curl up and hold your knees, keep ankles together, spin around once, then release, and you'll go in, feet first. Guaranteed."

Yeah, right. Ringling Brothers Circus is calling my cell right now.

Mudge said, "We might even live to tell about it."

"I'll show you how it's done, slugs!" shouted Jace. He anchored both fists above a knot and bounced on the limb before pushing off. The limb made a cracking sound.

"A-a-a-a-a-a-ah!" Jace yelled. He lost his grip. The rope slipped through his fingers. As he swayed and dangled, he tried to curl up, but there was no more rope. He plummeted to the water, arms and legs flying in all directions.

Smack!

Roaring laughter broke out. I felt a little sorry for Jace, even though I hated him. That landing had to hurt.

Jace surfaced, but kept his back to us.

"That was an amazing jump," called Mudge, still chuckling.

"I did it on purpose," said Jace, blowing out water through his nose. "Did I scare ya?"

"Yeah ya did, I'm so-o-o scared!" Biff busted out laughing again.

Jace joined them on the shore. "Okay, wise ass, it's your turn."

Biff scrambled back up the tree and checked the limb. I moved closer to the water's edge for a better view. He swung out, somersaulted in the air and landed a perfect one. So did Mudge. They'd had practice, but it took Skip and Capster three tries to get it right. Reggie, the brainiac, curled up and landed okay.

It was my chance. I could do this. Up the tree I went. At the top, I looked down. Skip waved and seemed so far away. I hoisted the rope. I grabbed above the knot and leaped.

At first, the glare on the water blinded me. Then the green trees growing on the opposite bank turned to blue sky. I was hanging in mid-air! I dropped the rope. I curled forward and gravity took over. My spin was lopsided because I could only grab one knee. Once around, I straightened out a little too late and hit the water like an open pair of scissors. I sank into the cool water, opened my eyes and kicked up to the sunny surface. It wasn't perfect. Would Jace let me pass?

"Aced it!" Skip clapped his hands.

Cheers burst out as I swam to the bank. I sure had good friends.

"I don't know," said Jace, shaking his head. "Looked pretty lame to me with your ankles so far apart."

Capster yelled, "Hey, it was more passable than your drop!"

"Come on," said Biff. "Have a heart."

"Yeah," added Mudge. "Give him a break."

Jace walked over with his hand extended. Was he going to congratulate me?

Instead, he spun and whacked my wet back. "I suppose it was good enough."

"Ouch!" I squeezed my shoulder blades together trying to stop the stinging. "Why'd you do that?"

"Because I can."

17
The Rotting Log

"Hang in there," whispered Skip. "His handprint is almost gone."

Jace hollered, "One more contest to go!"

All I had to do was conquer this last test to be a River Boy.

Reggie tapped Jace on the elbow. "What time is it?"

"Huh?" Jace screwed up his face. "How should I know?"

"Daytime!" said Mudge laughing.

"Where'd that come from, Reg?" I asked.

"I'm getting somewhat hungry, that's all."

"It's probably five o'clock," said Skip. "You can hang on a little longer."

Reggie rubbed his stomach. "I suppose I can."

"We should hurry anyway. We don't want to be discovered," said Skip. "It's risky to be here as it is."

"Head to the log," commanded Jace, searching his clothes pile, and then stuffing something red in his trunks.

We charged into the water. I was determined not to be last. Reggie lagged behind, which used to happen to little Billy all the time.

Jace dove under several times and bobbed up ahead of us.

What was he doing? I swam past his bubbles and stopped. My mind drifted to Billy.

"Come on, Ell," shouted Skip. "What are you waiting for?"

"Okay, okay." I backstroked to the log and scaled the roots to the top. No one spoke. Were they thinking about Billy, too?

Jace erupted in a volcano of water. His little red plastic ball floated next to him.

"What's that about?" asked Biff.

"Probably something death defying, knowing him," said Mudge.

I felt goose bumps spreading over me.

"Geez, how dangerous could a red plastic ball be?" asked Skip.

"Yeah, no big deal." Capster chimed in.

"Except this is the first time without Billy." I said as a chill ran up my spine.

"Just remember," said Skip. "Billy would've wanted us to have fun today, right?"

"Right!" Jace arrived and weaved between Biff and Capster sitting on the log's roots. At the top, he took his position again, King of the Hill. "That's the spirit."

Why did he have to mention spirits?

"Not only the usual running," said Jace, "but more."

"Uh-oh, for sure death defying," said Mudge.

"Yep," Jace walked out on the log, pointing a thumb over his shoulder. "See the famous Billy stub?"

We all nodded, slowly. Why did he have to give it Billy's name?

"Well, I'm going to stand there. You run full speed at me. I'll crouch and cup my hands. Put your left foot in my hands. I'll lift and pitch you as high as I can out over the water. Then dive."

"What's the catch?" I asked.

"Nothing. You just have to swim underwater and surface beyond that red ball floating over there."

I looked out at the red ball and gulped.

"That's incredibly far," said Reggie.

He took the words right out of my mouth.

"I know," said Jace. "Same routine. Three tries. I want the best guys in my club."

"I'll go first," said Capster.

I started wringing my hands. Wished I'd volunteered first, waiting only gave me more time to freak out.

Jace planted his feet near the stub, laced his fingers and yelled. "Okay!"

Capster raced out. Jace heaved him up. Capster dove and surfaced, looking around for the ball and gasping for air. "Did I?"

Jace shook his head. "You're short."

"How could I have missed?"

"The ball is behind you, dork. Next!" called Jace.

No one made it on the first try. After a second turn, only Capster succeeded. We gathered out in the water, grumbling.

Skip swam over to me. "Ask him to move the ball closer?"

"Me?" I asked. "You do it."

"He's your brother," said Skip.

"Yeah, like he's ever done anything for me."

"Always a first time," said Skip with a half-smile.

I didn't want to ask Jace for a favor, but I swam to the roots anyway, climbed out and sidestepped out onto the log to where the King of the Hill stood. Jace didn't pay attention to me. He cupped his hands around his mouth, ready to call the next contestant.

"What are you doing? You're not next." He grabbed my shoulders and whipped me around to his other side. He held me until I'd steadied myself. We faced each other, alone. Louder whooping and splashing filled the air.

"Now look, they've all scattered to a game of water tag," said Jace. "They'll never hear me call to get them organized again. You're in the way, you know that?" He started to cup his hands again.

"Wait. How about moving the ball a little closer this time?" I said. "Nobody can get out that far unless you give us a bigger and higher push off."

Jace was about to open his mouth.

"He can't. He's weak and can't lift you guys any higher," Duke called, standing on the log six feet away from Jace.

Where had he come from?

Jace slowly twisted around to face Duke. "So, you've decided to join us after all."

Duke shook his head. "Unfinished business, you might say."

"Later."

"No. Right now," said Duke in a deadly voice. "Nobody treats me like dirt and gets away with it. Not even you."

"Back off. My rules or get outta here." Jace faced the water and hollered, "Starting Round Three."

Duke took slo-mo steps toward Jace. Sunlight flashed off metal in his hand – a knife. As Duke lunged, I shoved Jace with all my might and his elbow caught me in the face. He spun, grabbing at me to catch his balance. Our hands clasped, but my hand slipped free.

"Damn you!" said Jace with hate in his eyes. He fell toward the water, gashing his head on the mossy log.

"Hey, something's happening!" shouted Biff, pointing at us. "Come on, guys." They all paddled at top speed toward us.

Deadman's Pocket

Duke moved toward me. I backed up fast. My feet slipped again and again until I tripped and fell hard onto Billy's stub.
Smack!

18

Did I Kill Again?

I came up for air. Breathing hurt. I had to get home. My right arm was useless, but reaching with my left, I sidestroked away from the log until I could touch bottom. My toes slipped in the mud. I fought to plow through chest deep water. I clawed up the bank and looked back. The boys had pulled Jace out, yelling and screaming.

"Were you trying to kill him?" shouted Biff in my direction.

"A-hole!" yelled Mudge at me.

None of them saw the knife like I did.

Jace was on all fours, coughing up water. Biff started wrapping Jace's bloody head with a beach towel.

Duke was nowhere to be seen.

My stomach lurched at the sight of Jace.

The boys scattered to get their clothes. Would they come after me? Searing pain shot through my arm. Holding it at my waist, I had a head start to my bike.

Halfway up the hill, I stopped. No voices. No crackling twigs behind me. The sudden replay of Duke's knife sent another jagged pain through me. The heat stifled my breathing, but I had to keep going.

I paused as I reached my bike. Mr. P waved to me from the tractor mower. I swayed, trying to wave back. Then I felt my face crash into the freshly cut lawn.

Everything went black.

19

Breaking the Rules

Skip hadn't answered any of my seven messages. I picked up my cell to redial when it vibrated.

"Where are you?" asked Skip.

"At home. I've been banished to my room till Dad gets home."

"So, what happened at the Pocket, dude?"

"I broke my arm and it's in a cast," I said, rubbing my swollen fingers.

"That sucks," said Skip.

'Yeah, and Jace got ten stitches in his head."

"Duke said you shoved Jace off the log," he said in a suspicious tone.

I bristled. "I only pushed Jace because Duke had a knife."

"No way!" said Skip.

"Don't you remember the one he pulled out that day he stole the comic book at Curry's Pharmacy?"

"Are you sure?" His voice made it clear he didn't believe my story.

"I'm not blind!" I growled.

"Why would Duke pull a knife on his best friend?"

"I dunno."

"It doesn't add up," said Skip. "It's crazy."

I clenched my fists. "I'm telling you, Duke was mad when he came at Jace. I couldn't let him stab my brother. I didn't even think twice–I just pushed."

"So you hurt Jace instead," said Skip, confused.

"I didn't mean to! I was trying to get Jace away from Duke's knife." If Skip wouldn't believe me, then who would?

"I'd say you're busted for sure," said Skip.

"Big help you are." I wished he'd quit giving me a hard time. He sounded like my Dad. I paused for a second before changing the subject. "Miss O' called. She gave my solo to Marcy."

"You'll never hear the end of it from Missy Redhead," said Skip.

"Hey, it's not like I didn't know she'd get it. When I skipped rehearsal I *gave* it to her."

"Oops, gotta go. My mom's calling me. Good luck." Skip hung up.

Did he believe me or not? I had tried to tell Mom at the hospital what happened, but she was too hysterical. And she didn't want to hear anything from either of us until Dad got home. It was torture waiting for Dad. I stared at my bedroom ceiling.

An hour later, Dad's car pulled into the driveway. He stormed into the house, slamming doors and yelling for Jace and me to get to the living room. When I arrived he was pacing in front of the fireplace, hands clasped behind his back. Mom stood next to him with her arms crossed. Her pursed lips and the deep creases on Dad's forehead meant this was going to be bad.

I sat on the sofa. Like a pig at slaughter, I waited for my life to come to an end. Jace shuffled in and plopped down as far away from me as he could, his ten stitches giving him ten more reasons to hate me.

Dad came to a halt facing Jace and me. "What were you two thinking?" He shouted. "Were you trying to kill yourselves? You were forbidden to go to the swimming hole. Have you already forgotten what happened to Billy?" The blood vessels in his neck looked ready to burst. "Jason, I'm so disappointed in you. As the oldest, I would have expected you to stop this nonsense. You should have been more responsible."

I snickered. If Dad only knew – being there was Jace's idea.

Dad glared at me.

Mom came closer. "Duke's father called. He said that Duke saw Elliot shove Jason." She looked ready to cry. "He said Elliot was a danger to society."

My jaw dropped open. "Me? A danger? I didn't do anything—I mean—I did—but it wasn't my fault!"

Jace cracked a smile. "Yeah right, Squeaky."

"This isn't funny," barked Dad. "I want the truth." He frowned at each of us in turn.

Finally, a chance to tell my side of the story! I cleared my throat. "I, uh—"

"It was a club," blurted Jace.

Dad raised an eyebrow. "What kind of club?"

"The River Boys Club," said Jace. "I wanted to get the guys together and have some fun." Jace clamped his hands in his armpits. "Everyone was so bummed after Billy's accident. We needed to go back there and get over being scared of the place before you guys chopped the log to pieces. I mean, the hole has been a playground for generations around here, including for you, Sir. Besides, kids need to get out and exercise, right? Everyone thought it was an awesome idea and I wanted to be the leader."

My mouth hung open again.

"So I set up some tests," said Jace.

"Why did you need to do that?" asked Dad.

"It's the only way to have a respectable club."

How could Jace, who seemed to be enjoying himself, think he'd skate past Dad with such an explanation? I wondered if Dad would be pissed?

"The tests were cool, like carrying rocks underwater, somersaulting from the rope swing and running the slimy log. You know, tests to prove they could handle Deadman's Pocket.

You'd have liked it. It would prove how tough they could be."

"Deadman's Pocket?" asked Dad.

"I named it because Billy was dead," said Jace, beaming. "Cool name, huh?"

If only Jace could hear himself. Dad started pacing again while Jace kept right on digging himself a deeper hole.

"My club was gonna be exclusive. Only the strongest and bravest kids would get in. I gave each kid three tries, and most needed 'em all, too. If they made it, they'd be ready for anything."

I couldn't believe I'd given up my solo for this.

"I mean, it's good to be brave and have character, isn't it? That's what you always taught me about the Marines." Jace peered up at his dad. "I thought I was helping these guys stand up and be prepared. Semper Fi, Sir."

I half-expected my brother to salute right then.

But silence.

Jace looked down and mumbled. "Nobody said we couldn't have a club."

"The swimming hole was off limits," said Dad in a tight voice. "That was a serious mistake in judgment."

Jace paused. "Yes, Sir."

"What made you think it would be okay?" asked Dad.

"Once you saw how much fun we were having, I thought it wouldn't have mattered. Nobody got hurt until Squeaky here," Jace pointed a thumb toward me, "went and shoved me for no reason."

"What about you, Elliot?" demanded Dad, getting redder in the face. "You disobeyed my orders, too. You also missed a supposedly important rehearsal, and hurt your brother. Do you want to tell me why I shouldn't ground you until you're twenty-one?"

My heart banged against my ribs. "I was just tryin–"

The doorbell rang. Everyone exchanged glances.

"Hold on a minute, Elliot," said Dad.

Mom went to answer the door. I slumped back into the sofa cushions, which made my arm ache more. Jace leaned forward, cradling his head in his hands.

Mom cleared her throat. We all turned to the doorway. A huge policeman stood next to my Mom, dwarfing her.

Was I going to be arrested?

Suddenly, out from behind the blue uniform popped Marcy's head.

"Hi, Elliot!"

20

Out of the Blue

"Hello, Mr. Wermann. I'm Detective Ramirez." The officer walked over to shake Dad's hand. Marcy followed the cop like a puppy. What was she doing here? Mom scurried over and stood close to Dad.

"Pardon the intrusion," the detective glanced at Jace and me, "but a serious situation developed this afternoon."

Maybe he was here to read me my rights. I swallowed hard.

"Remember when the town council voted to install a fence blocking access to the swimming hole?" asked the detective.

"Of course I do. I was at that meeting and spoke in favor of it," said Dad.

"Later, the council also authorized a fine for trespassing."

Penalty? If that was true, no allowance until I turned twenty-five. I felt queasy.

"I see," said Dad

"Yes," said the detective. "Though we never anticipated we'd have to enforce it."

"What are you saying?" asked Mom, looking worried.

The detective continued. "A very irritated Mr. Dukovny called this afternoon. Apparently, some boys went to the swimming hole today because your son, Jason, lured them into breaking the law, which resulted in injuries."

Dad inhaled his words through clenched teeth. "We were just discussing that very situation." He exhaled. "I'll make sure my boys pay their fines. Seems Elliot had a lot to do with this." His eyes drilled through me.

Then Marcy winked at me!

The officer hooked his thumbs into his leather belt. "Mr. Wermann, I believe in getting all the facts before writing tickets for fines. If you don't mind, I want you to hear this." The detective nodded to Marcy. "Go ahead, young lady, tell your story."

Marcy winked at me again. She twirled the end of her red-haired ponytail between her fingers.

Usually, I ignored her every word. But not this time.

"I was on the rock ledge and saw everything," said Marcy. "See, after Elliot missed rehearsal, I went to find him and tell him Miss O' gave me his solo. I knew exactly where he'd be—all the kids knew about the "secret" tryouts. When I got to the swimming hole, they'd already started. So I hid up on the rock ledge and watched." She glared at Jace. "I wanted to go to the tryouts, but no girls were allowed. You know, I could have aced every contest. I'm stronger and have more guts than Reggie and Skip put together. And..."

"All right, Marcy," said the detective. "Stick to the story."

"Yes Sir." She dug her toe into the carpet, then started right up again. "Anyway, from up high like I was, I watched Harold Dukovny, also known as Duke, Sir."

"Thank you, Marcy," said the detective. "Please continue."

"Okay. So, Jace and Elliot were out on the log. Then Duke climbed up, too. I saw him pull something out of his pocket. Then he walked out toward Jace."

I sucked in air and held my breath.

Marcy acted out her story. "Well, he flicked his wrist. He had a knife. I saw it 'cuz the sun reflected off it."

Jace piped up. "He did not. You're lying."

"Let her finish," said the detective.

Marcy went on with her theatrics. "Next thing I knew, Duke lunged. Jace never saw the knife coming, but Elliot must have. Before I could scream, Elliot shoved Jace off the log, making Elliot lose his balance. Then I saw Duke drop the knife into the water." She faced Jace, wagging her finger at him. "You could have died! You're lucky your brother saved you."

Jace stared at Marcy in disbelief.

She looked at me. "Sorry you got hurt, Elliot."

Marcy was amazing!

Then she dropped her arms to her sides. "That's when I ran to the police to tell them what I saw."

I struggled to stand. "Marcy's right! That's what I've been trying to tell you!"

"Why would Duke do that?" asked Jace, shaking his head. "She must be wrong."

Crossing her arms over her chest, Marcy stomped her foot. "I'm telling the truth!"

Dad screwed up his face. "Has this been verified?"

"Yes," said the detective. "After Marcy's report, the chief sent my partner and me to the swimming hole. We found the knife exactly where she said it would be. When we returned, we found the station filled with angry parents led by Mr. Dukovny. Because of Jason's alleged role as the ringleader, Mr. Dukovny is demanding Jason pay the fines for all the boys, including Elliot."

Dad rubbed his chin, several times. "Is that man out of his mind?"

Mom's hands flew to her mouth. "That could be a lot of money!"

"Yes, ma'am," said the detective.

Jace's eyes seemed glued open as far as they could stretch, never blinking. Mom staggered to the armchair.

"Paying for all the boys?" asked Dad. "That's ridiculous."

"During the uproar at the station," said the detective. "Duke accused Elliot of pushing Jason off the log –"

"That's when I blasted the creep!" said Marcy.

"Yes, you set the record straight, Marcy," said the detective. "Michael, I think he's nicknamed Skip, stepped forward and said he'd seen Duke flash his knife a few days ago, behind Curry's Pharmacy."

Mom jumped out of her chair. "Oh my God!" She circled the chair holding her forehead then plopped back down.

Jace collapsed on the sofa. "What's going to happen to Duke now?"

"That's why I'm here." The detective took out his notepad and turned to Mom and Dad. "No fines, but do you want to press assault charges against Harold or...er...Duke?"

"Awesome, Dad, press charges!" I shouted. Finally, the jerk would be where he belonged, behind bars.

Mom stood up, wringing her hands. "Kenneth, I need a moment to think."

"What's to think about, Frances?" asked Dad, tapping his foot. "The kid nearly stabbed Jason and blamed Elliot for it."

Deadman's Pocket

She moved closer to Dad and whispered something in his ear. The room went silent while they paused with their heads together.

Now what?

"Detective," said Dad quietly. "If I ever want another one of my favorite blueberry pies, we will have to get back to you."

The cop dug out a business card and handed it to Dad. "Sure thing. Here's my number, but please call me before noon. Mr. Dukovny is understandably worried. Come along, Marcy. I need to get you home."

Marcy nodded then walked over to me, batting her thick eyelashes. "Can I be the first one to sign your cast?"

"Sure." I laughed in relief. I'd let her do anything now.

Marcy pulled her Sharpie from her pocket. She drew a heart and wrote in big fat letters:

ELLIOT, MY HERO!

21

Brothers

Mom walked Detective Ramirez and Marcy to the door.

"Elliot," said Dad.

I traced Marcy's cool writing on my cast. I still couldn't believe how she'd helped me.

"Elliot!" shouted Dad, causing me to flinch.

"Um...Sir?"

"Both of you to your rooms," said Dad. "Your mother and I need to a talk."

Jace was halfway up the stairs before I hefted myself off the sofa. Not a peep or squawk came from his room. I flipped on the light in my room. A breeze fluttered the curtains. I sat on the edge of my bed, listening to the crickets outside. I sighed. At least now the truth was out thanks to Marcy.

I lay back on my bed. What was in store for me now? I hoped Jace would get a major punishment because his RBC tryouts had gotten everyone into trouble. Dad had better not cut Jace any slack this time. One thing was sure. Once Dad made up his mind that was it. "Suck it up and take it like a man," he always said.

I turned on the classical radio station, but I lost interest and quickly turned it off. I closed my eyes and hummed my solo or rather Marcy's solo. After coming to my rescue, she deserved it even more.

I could only hear Mom and Dad's faint mumbling downstairs. I scooted out of bed, went to the door and turned the knob. There stood Jace, barefoot, pressing his hands against his temples. His face looked gray.

Was he here to tell me again how much he hated me?

"I've been thinking about what Marcy said about Duke. If the detective and everybody else believes her, then I guess I should too." Jace dropped his hands and stood there, wobbling. "Ever since Duke's mom ran out on his dad, he's been ready to explode. I knew he had lots of problems so I ignored what a jerk he was. I didn't think he'd turn on me." I sat on my bed and Jace collapsed beside me. "Ell, if you hadn't skipped rehearsal and been on that log, I could have been really hurt or dead." Jace's eyes got wet. "Thanks for being a great brother." He flung an arm around my neck—a Jace-style hug. "And if I'd known Duke had threatened you behind Curry's Pharmacy, I'd have dragged him to the cops myself."

"*Really?*" My chest swelled.

"No one messes with my little brother, but me." Jace tussled up my hair and laughed.

I started to crack a smile.

"Seriously," said Jace. "I'll never forget what you did. Ever." He held up his fist and we bumped.

I felt like I had a brother for the first time.

Dad's voice boomed up the stairs. "Boys, come on down."

We stared at each other, knowing what was next. After everything Jace had just said, I was sorry I'd wished a worse punishment on him.

Jace led the way. We took our seats again on the sofa. Dad pulled up the ottoman in front of us and sat down, rubbing his thighs.

"So, what punishment do you think you deserve?" asked Dad, leaning in and glaring at us.

"Whatever you decide, Sir," said Jace. "But go easy on Elliot. He saved my life. I'd caused the problem and I'm very sorry for that, Sir." Jace winced and cradled his head in his hands again.

Dad straightened up then peered at me. "And you, Elliot?"

I stared at Dad's shoes, rocking back and forth. "I know I disobeyed your orders, Sir, and I should have gone to rehearsal. You pay a lot of money for my violin lessons." At that moment, I looked him square in the eye. "But I'm not sorry one bit for what I did, Sir." I rubbed my shoulder.

"Your mother and I are upset that you both disobeyed," said Dad. "Elliot, even though you ducked out on your rehearsal, which was wrong, you ended up being in the right place at the right time. What you did was brave, Son. I'm proud of you."

I couldn't believe my ears. Dad was proud of me! Me!

Dad continued. "Jason, did you really think I'd buy all that baloney about helping the younger boys get over their fears?"

Jace bowed his head.

"Still though," said Dad. "Regarding your punishments..."

The pause seemed like forever.

"Your mother and I think you've learned your lessons."

My chest sagged as I exhaled.

"There's more," said Dad, "We decided not to press charges against Duke."

"Don't I have a say in this?" protested Jace. "He's so guilty!"

"We know," said Dad. "Duke's actions were reprehensible, but we felt he needs help more than Juvenile Hall. His father agreed to have Duke perform one hundred hours of community service work."

Whoa! A hundred hours. I could see Duke now, picking up dog poop, emptying trash bins along Main Street or planting flowers with Mr. P in the park.

"Jason, we think you should offer some community service time right here at home," said Dad.

Jace groaned. "What do you mean?"

Dad continued, "As soon as your stitches come out, I've volunteered you to help me paint the house."

I smiled. "I'll hold the paint bucket!"

22

4th of July

The 4th of July crowds crammed into every picnic area in Jasper Lawton Ipes Park. The traveling carnival set up a miniature ferris wheel in the parking lot and sold sticky cotton candy. The baseball diamonds, swing sets and teeter-totters were never empty. Barbecue smells and blue smoke filled the air. Dad grilled our burgers. Skip and I ate till our bellies ached. Jace helped the firefighters sell their famous Red Hot Chili. Jace tipped his chef's hat at me every time Skip and I strolled past the booth as we criss-crossed the park. Fathers played baseball. Mothers entered the pie contests. The little kids stumbled around in burlap sack races.

I looked around for Marcy but didn't see her anywhere.

At dusk, the flashing neon lights on the ferris wheel lit up. It was almost time for the concert. Skip and I headed over to stake out a spot. Mom and Dad hung out with their friends at the refreshment shack.

We plopped down on the grass close to the gazebo. The new stage was decked out with red, white and blue streamers and buntings. Helium-filled balloons jostled at the end of taut ribbons.

Soon Capster and Reggie joined us.

"Too bad you can't solo," said Reggie.

I shrugged. "Next year."

"But he has a good reason," said Skip. "Pretty hard to play with that big white thing on his arm."

"Most certainly," said Reggie, pushing up his glasses.

Jace showed up with Biff and Mudge. We bunched up to make room for them.

"Weren't you all blown away to find out what happened out there on the log?" asked Skip, glancing at everyone. "Lucky to have Elliot around."

"Remarkable bravery," said Reggie.

"Yep," said Jace, placing his hand on my good shoulder.

I beamed.

"So Jace, what about RBC?" asked Capster, turning the conversation serious.

"RBC's dead in the water," said Jace.

"Hey, didn't you see the newspaper on Sunday?" asked Skip.

Who could miss the huge article about the log removal? The color photos of Nick, his chainsaw and the growing pile of oak firewood hogged the entire front page.

Jace continued, "I've learned my lesson. If Squea—uh-- Elliot hadn't been there, I might not be here. We were messin' around in a dangerous place. Time to move on."

"To what?" asked Mudge. "Jumping off the rock ledge was cool."

"So was the rope swing," said Biff. "I think we should..."

Jace reached over and yanked on Biff's T-shirt. "Give it a rest."

Biff raised his palms in surrender, "Okay, okay!"

"Speaking of moving on, I heard Duke is leaving town," said Mudge.

"Says who?" asked Skip.

"My mom," said Mudge. "She works at the bank and helped Duke's father close his account yesterday."

"Where are they going?" asked Biff.

"Texas," said Mudge, "Apparently, his father has a new job there."

"What about his hundred hours of community service?" I asked.

"I guess he'll have to finish them up somewhere else," said Jace.

Mudge inspected my cast. "You need some stuff written on that thing. Hey Reg, gotta pen?"

Reggie smiled and pulled out his trusty Sharpie.

Shirley Manis

Mudge gently lifted my plastered arm and found Marcy's message. "Who wrote: 'Elliot My Hero!' with the heart?"

"Oo-oo-oo, somebody likes you!" teased Mudge.

"Wouldn't be Marcy, would it?" asked Capster.

Skip nodded. "I think he likes her back, too."

"I can't help what she writes on my cast," I said.

Taking turns, they scribbled their messages but I didn't let anyone close to Marcy's writing.

The audience gathered behind us.

Suddenly, a big drum roll rumbled from the back of the orchestra. I loved drum rolls because that meant something interesting was about to happen. The musicians filed onto the stage and stood at attention. Marcy came on last, as the first chair violinist, leader of the orchestra always did. She was wearing a blue dress, white sandals and her shiny red hair was neatly braided. I couldn't hold back my smile. With a huge cymbal crash, Old Glory unfurled and dropped from the roof behind the orchestra.

The crowd erupted into deafening applause. The mayor tapped the microphone until everyone quieted down.

"LADIES AND GENTLEMEN," boomed the mayor. "WELCOME TO THE ANNUAL 4th OF JULY CONCERT!"

The crowd applauded again. Jace whistled through his teeth.

The mayor extended his arms trying to bring silence.

"Without further adieu, folks, I give you Miss O'Looney, superb music teacher and outstanding conductor of the combined Vermont orchestras of Taftsville and Woodstock middle schools!"

More applause broke out.

Miss O' smiled widely, bowed twice, then took her place at the microphone. "Good evening! First of all, a big thank you to the parents for making this performance possible. Without your support and all the bake sales and silent auctions, we would not have a music program. And, a special congratulations to these students who take music seriously and have prepared tonight's exciting program. We hope you enjoy the performance."

Parents popped up with cell phone cameras as Miss O' turned and swooped her baton, signaling the orchestra to take a bow.

Was Marcy nervous? Should I wave? But she gazed out over our heads. I remembered what it felt like. The whole town was focused on her, including me. She stepped up to the microphone, and said, "Please stand for our National Anthem." Miss O' swooped her baton toward the musicians.

The Anthem began. I placed my hand over my heart with everyone else and sang along. Marcy's big moment was approaching. All the violin bows bobbed in unison. Soon she would carry the melody alone. That's when she looked my way and winked. Then her violin soared.

"And the rockets red glare..."

I smiled, my fingers playing along with Marcy. She was perfect. Her eight-measure solo was over in a flash. The orchestra grew louder and the audience belted out the words. *"Oh, say does that star-spangled banner yet wave, O'er the land of the free and the home of the brave!"*

Miss O' held her arms extra wide, holding the last note. Everyone applauded. Marcy grinned at me. Roaring whoops and cheers. Marcy waved her bow at me. I gave her a thumb up. She smiled back. I pumped my good fist over my head.

"That was awesome," shouted Skip, clapping like a circus seal.

I couldn't have agreed more. She looked at me when she wasn't reading music. I gazed at her, watching every blink of her lush eyelashes. She was a daredevil who told the truth for me and she played my solo as well as I could have. Marcy was gorgeous and amazing.

Then Miss O' then took the microphone. "And now, our finale will be *Stars and Stripes Forever* by John Philip Sousa."

The brass led off the march with a couple of sour notes, but no one cared. We leaped to our feet, and high-stepped to the march.

At the last refrain, Marcy stepped forward. With a sweeping arm motion, she aimed her bow over our heads toward the baseball field. The lights dimmed.

Thup! Thup! Thup! Fireworks exploded. Sparkling, sizzling and crackling ones sprayed red, white and blue glitter across the night sky. The thunderous booms rattled my chest. The display lasted for ten minutes. Ten incredible minutes.

Afterward, we all huddled together to say our good-byes. I turned toward the stage, but all the musicians had cleared out. I craned my neck looking for Marcy. Then someone tapped me on the shoulder. It was Marcy.

I smiled. "You were terrific!"

"Do you really think so?" said Marcy, tugging at the side seams of her dress.

"Way to go, Marcy!" said Skip and Capster in unison.

"Such a virtuoso," remarked Reggie.

I moved sideways, widening the circle for her. "Hey, maybe we could include her in our next—"

"I have an even better idea," said Marcy.

Jace, Biff, Mudge, Skip, Capster, Reggie and I stopped talking and our ears perked.

"Have you guys ever tried the Zip Line in Smuggler's Notch State Park?"

"I'm in!" I said as all of us did high fives.

Epilogue

Elliot
In His Own Words

My name is Elliot D. Wermann. I was born on September 4, 2009 at the Naval Hospital, Camp Pendleton, California, because that's where my Dad, Sergeant Kenneth D. Wermann, was stationed. Dad said he passed out cigars and was a proud Marine Dad that day. Mom said she cried happy tears. My hair is still blonde and my eyes are deep blue.

Dad named me Elliot for Camp Elliot, the first home of his 9th Marine Regiment near San Diego. He told me when Camp Pendleton opened, the Camp Elliot troops marched the 35 miles north to their new Camp Pendleton, instead of getting a ride in trucks. President Franklin Delano Roosevelt officially dedicated Camp Pendleton on September 25, 1942. Mom gave his middle name. So, I'm Elliot Delano Wermann. My parents named me after a stupid marine camp and a crippled president.

My brother Jason is three years older than me. My Dad named Jason for the months July-August-September-October and November. That was so cool. He was given Emerson as a middle name for no particular reason. I just know Jace hates it. All my grandparents are dead, except Grandma Weston. She's old and lives in a nursing home in Boston.

Jace plays tricks on me, calls me names and picks fights. Once he told me sausages were made of mashed up cow noses. I don't know why he said that. He says I bug him to death. Well, I do, sometimes, but not all the time. It just proves he's hated me since I was born.

I was 5 years old when we moved to Camp Lejeune in North Carolina. I remember Mom crying about moving. She hated moving. Dad got promoted and became a good Marine captain.

Two summers ago when I was 10, Dad said he wanted us to live like civilians. He decided on Taftsville, Vermont. He didn't ask Mom, Jace or me. Mom cried when we had to move. She dried her eyes and I helped her pack.

My mom, Frances Bernice Weston Wermann, works part-time as a waitress at the Acorn Café. I don't think she makes much money. I know because I've peeked into her wallet once hoping she'd have a few quarters for a slushie. Even when she's tired she helps me with homework and violin lessons. She can really cook, too. I love her stir-fry.

When I hear my parents arguing it makes my stomach upset. It's usually over something Jace did. Dad blames her for not being strict enough. I try to get Jace in trouble whenever Dad is at home. He never seems to get it that Jace is turning into a bad guy. Jace gets away with a lot.

The first week in my new hometown, I met Mr. Pazaropoulos, the cemetery gardener, who has been like a grandpa to me. My own Dad doesn't talk to me as much as Mr. P does. He listens to my problems. His English isn't so good, but I like to hear the stories about his mountain village in Greece.

My best friend is Skip, or Michael Barnhart, who lives next door. Skip's upstairs bedroom window faces mine. We could shout to each other, but he still calls or texts my cell phone. We made friends with Capster, known as Carl Pananelli, nicknamed for his baseball cap antics. Reggie, known as Reginald Moss III, was the smartest kid in the whole school. And, Billy Martin, the kid everyone liked the most. Skip's mother is nice. His father smokes a pipe. I cough a lot around him. Skip's little sister Marianna, asks "Why?" too much and gets into all kinds of mischief.

Skip and I ride our bikes all around town.

I've never lived in a house with stairs or a basement. Upstairs, Jace has a bigger bedroom. Doesn't matter to me. Less room to clean if I do clean it. I don't have to put up with Jace bouncing quarters off his blanket anymore like when we shared a bedroom. Jace's room is like Neatsville. He lines up his books from tallest to shortest, hangs up his clothes so the hangers all face the same way, and polishes his shoes. He screams if I even touch his doorknobs. He drives me crazy. But Jace is good at sports, especially baseball. I wish Dad would coach me like he coaches Jace.

In my bedroom, I leave a music stand up and stacked with practice books. I wish I had a bigger desk. When the piles get too high, I just sweep my arm across the top to clear it. Throwing dirty clothes under my bed gets them out of the way. Last week I had to pay an overdue fine for a library book that accidentally slid under my bed. That dumb book cost me a week's allowance!

I love playing the violin. Someday I want to solo at New York's Carnegie Hall or hear violinist Itzhak Perlman play in person. If Mom knew I was pitching baseball, she'd get a headache. I need to practice in case Dad ever wants to play catch with me. But I bet he never will.

My middle school teachers were pretty and smelled of perfume. I loved it when Mom came to school for open house and my orchestra recitals. I can't remember Dad ever coming to school for a visit. Not even on "What Does Your Dad Do?" days when he was home.

A couple months ago I caught Jace and his buddy, Duke, smoking at the swimming hole. I found some cigarette butts and match sticks in the bushes on the rock ledge. I've hidden that proof in our garage. If he bugs me anymore, I'm telling Dad.

Before the Billy accident, the one good thing about Taftsville was the swimming hole. In the summer heat, it was the place to cool off. The other good thing was that I learned to swim at Deadman's Pocket.

Jace
In His Own Words

My name is Jason E. Wermann. I was born on December 25, 2006 at the Naval Hospital, Camp Pendleton, California. My father, Sergeant Kenneth D. Wermann, was stationed at Camp Pendleton. He's a Marine and proud of it. When my father first saw me he said I was some Christmas present! He named me for the months he was away on assignment by taking the first letter of July-August-September-October and November. I became Jason. My mom picked her father's name, Emerson, for my middle name who died before I was born. I hate the stupid name, even though Mom said he was smart and invented stuff. I inherited my father's brown hair and blue eyes.

Grandma Weston is my only living grandma. She's pretty old. Sometimes Mom forces me to talk to her on the phone, but the old lady never hears what I say. My father's parents died a long time ago.

For three years I was the only kid then my brother was born. My father named him Elliot for Camp Elliot. I'm the one who wants to be Marine

Shirley Manis

someday. That name should have been mine. Mom told me I was mad about getting a brother and that I tried to snuff Elliot out with a pillow. She said she caught me and ruined my attack. Unfortunately, he's still alive and the idiot has been buggin' me ever since.

When I was 8 years old my father was sent to Camp Lejeune in North Carolina for training and a chance for a promotion. He did well and soon became Captain Wermann.

Our new base had lots of kids, all ages, and a cool playground. I got plenty of cuts and scrapes, but I just spit on the wounds and kept playing. The kids thought I was tough. My father coached our baseball team. He taught me how to pitch, hit and catch a baseball. He put me on first base every game and got mad whenever I dropped the ball. I worked hard to make him proud of me. I wanted to be the best first baseman ever, unlike Elliot. He's a lousy baseball player with two left feet and can't hit a target. He's useless.

The military school on the base was boring. My grades barely passed. Elliot always did better than me. I mostly remember Mr. Kimes, my 4th grade teacher. He paddled me in the principal's office once for writing the F-word in chalk on the sidewalk. He had a strong swing. I vowed never to get caught again.

We moved to Taftsville two summers ago. My father quit the military and became an insurance salesman. I'll never know why he picked this place. His first huge mistake, but here we are in a little Vermont town.

At least we have a bigger house. I finally have my own room. I pinned up posters of my baseball heroes Hank Aaron and Babe Ruth. I like my clothes hung in the closet, dress shoes polished, and my bed blankets tucked tight enough to bounce a quarter. My father said I'd make a great Marine. On the other hand, Elliot is a regular slob. His room stinks to hell. Mom never tells me what a clean room I have. She doesn't say one word about Elliot's garbage dump. She gives the little twerp extra rope all the time. He's a weakling, too. That's why it's so easy to get him into trouble.

I walk everywhere I want to go.

My father looks handsome in his uniform. My father says a uniform was a good way to catch girls, but soldiers have to go to basic training and get up before dawn. I'm glad I don't have to do that yet. My father travels a lot for his job and leaves me in charge and tells me to suck it up like a man. I do and I forgive him for dumping us in this little town.

My mom, Frances Wermann, works part-time at the Acorn Cafe. She said her paycheck helps pay the bills. I saw the mortgage bill once. It's a whopping fortune. She's tired and crabby sometimes, and never seems to have time to help me with my homework. She has plenty of time for Elliot, the squeaky violinist. She's a good cook but some nights she brings home food from the cafe.

I get bored around the house and I don't like TV. When my father is away for his job, I wait until Mom falls asleep, then I sneak out my bedroom window. I meet my buddies Mudge and Biff, also known as Mudson and Bifford. We hang out under the streetlights near the drugstore.

My best buddy is Duke. His real name is Franklin Dukovny. His family is rich and he has lived in Taftsville since he was born. Duke and I became best friends right away. Once he dared me to steal a pen from the drugstore. I did. It was a breeze. Now, we go back there and take turns stealing. Duke and I stole some beer from the 7-Eleven during school lunch break. The principal called Mom and she had to bail Duke and me out of his office. Mom wants me to ditch Duke as a friend, but I won't. Duke is brave and thinks up dangerous stuff to do.

Both Duke and I like listening to Hip-Hop and hide out at the swimming hole to smoke. Duke steals lighters and cigarettes from his father's supply. If Elliot knew, he'd tell. If my father found out, I'd be grounded for the rest of my life.

Elliot would never smoke. He's a Mr. Goody-Goody. Even if he got caught, he'd use his famous

Deadman's Pocket

line, "What did I do?" It bugs the hell out of me that he gets so many second chances.

Mom doesn't report stuff I do to my father. She can't win an argument with him, either. My father is always in command.

I don't have a girlfriend like some guys. With a girlfriend, you have to go over to her house, sit with her family and watch TV. I'd rather spend time with Duke.

The best thing about Taftsville was the swimming hole. The River Boys Club would have been so cool if Duke hadn't gone crazy with his knife.

Shirley Manis

About the Author

Shirley Manis lives on the Central Coast of California with Rosie, her Maltipoo.